"What...what are

The words came out a little breathless, egging him on in ways he couldn't begin to describe. "Payback."

"Ethan, I'm warning you—"

"Yeah, yeah, heard that before." Blinking snow out of his eyes, he gave Flicka a sidelong glance. "Hey, kid, want to learn how to make a perfect snow angel?"

"I do, I do, I do."

"Good news. Keely has agreed to demonstrate the proper technique."

She gasped. "Ethan, no. Don't. I...I'm..."

"You...you're...what?"

"Cold." Keely said the word triumphantly, as if she'd come up with the last clue in a difficult crossword puzzle.

"Nothing like a little physical activity to warm you up. Trust me on this," he whispered in her ear. "I'm a doctor."

He hooked his foot around the back of her knees and, grinning, dumped her gently into the snow.

Flat on her back, she gaped up at him three entire seconds. "You will pay for this."

It was both a challenge and a promise. The woman made him smile.

Renee Ryan grew up in a Florida beach town where she learned to surf, sort of. With a degree from FSU, she explored career opportunities at a Florida theme park and a modeling agency and even taught high school economics. She currently lives with her husband in Nebraska, and many have mistaken their overweight cat for a small bear. You may contact Renee at reneeryan.com, on Facebook or on Twitter, @ReneeRyanBooks.

Books by Renee Ryan

Love Inspired

Village Green

Claiming the Doctor's Heart
The Doctor's Christmas Wish

Love Inspired Historical

Charity House

The Marshal Takes a Bride
Hannah's Beau
Loving Bella
The Lawman Claims His Bride
Charity House Courtship
The Outlaw's Redemption
Finally a Bride
His Most Suitable Bride
The Marriage Agreement

Visit the Author Profile page at Harlequin.com for more titles.

The Doctor's Christmas Wish

Renee Ryan

Recycling programs for this product may not exist in your area.

 ™ LOVE INSPIRED BOOKS

ISBN-13: 978-0-373-81879-2

The Doctor's Christmas Wish

www.Harlequin.com

Printed in U.S.A.

Trust in the Lord with all your heart and lean not on your own understanding; in all your ways submit to Him, and He will make your paths straight.
—*Proverbs* 3:5–6

To my fabulous, incredibly smart, savvy editor, Melissa Endlich. I'll treasure your kindness, insight and generosity for many years to come. You deserve only the best in life.

Chapter One

The house phone rang at 10:33 p.m. on the Sunday after Thanksgiving. The high-pitched sound yanked Ethan Scott's attention away from the television screen and the football game he'd carved out time to watch live, no distractions.

Who would be calling at this hour?

The hitch in his breath was born out of a hidden fear he kept tucked deep inside his soul. When his parents were killed in a fatal car crash, Ethan had been the first to get the news. As the oldest of four, he had to identify the bodies, to inform his three younger siblings and to handle all the funeral arrangements.

He'd completed each task without hesitation, and had been forced to repeat an eerily similar process a year and a half ago when another deadly car accident had taken his fiancée.

The incessant ringing continued.

Like a shock wave, old memories rippled across new. Ethan's previously easy, relaxed mood spiraled into something darker.

He debated ignoring the call. Few people had his home number, and any medical emergency would either go to his answering service or come through on his cell phone.

The ringing stopped.

Banishing unwanted memories and the emotions they brought, Ethan sat back to enjoy the game. The Broncos were about to score a touchdown.

The ringing started up again.

Ethan's gut took a hard roll. Surely the Lord wouldn't deal him another blow, wouldn't make him suffer through another unexpected goodbye. He'd had enough sorrow for one lifetime. He put the game on mute, then made the short trek from living room to kitchen.

The sound of doggy toenails clicking on the tile floor alerted him that his treasured black Lab had followed him. He patted Baloo on the head and then glanced at the caller ID.

Keely O'Toole. Ethan's gut took another hard roll, for an entirely different reason this time.

His neighbor was one of the few women in town he tended to avoid, for reasons he didn't want to explore tonight. Or ever.

Since Keely made a habit of avoiding him as well, he figured whatever had incited her to call the house—twice—on the landline—had to be important.

He snatched up the telephone receiver. "Ethan speaking."

A short, tense pause sounded on the other end of the line, followed by a weary female sigh. "Is Ryder around? He's not answering his cell phone."

"Hello to you, too, Keely."

She sighed again, the sound filled with frustration. "Is Ryder home or not?"

"Not. He's working the night shift at the hospital."

"That's unfortunate."

Something in her voice put Ethan on alert. He could practically feel Keely's agitation coming through the phone. Both his younger brothers were doctors. But where Ethan was a primary care physician and Brody was working for Doctors Without Borders, Ryder specialized in emergency medicine.

If she was calling Ryder this late at night...

"Talk to me, Keely. What's going on?"

"I need your help."

Four words Ethan never expected to come out the woman's mouth, at least not directed at him.

Something must be seriously wrong. "Are you hurt?"

"It's not me. It's Felicity. She's really sick and I don't know what to do. Should I take her out in this weather, to the ER waiting room, or do I hold off, pray it'll go away? I'm really, really worried."

She was also rambling. Another first.

Ethan mentally sorted through her words, stopping on an unfamiliar name. *Felicity.* Who was Felicity? His mind went blank. Then he remembered the little girl who had moved in with Keely over the holiday weekend. He didn't know the whole story, only that Keely was the child's legal guardian for an indefinite amount of time.

"What's wrong with her?"

"She's complaining of stomach pain."

In full doctor mode now, Ethan digested this piece of information. "Any vomiting?"

"Just once, about an hour ago."

"When did she last eat?"

"Around six."

He checked his watch, did a mental calculation between regular dinner hours and now. "What did she eat?"

"A hamburger, fries, oh, and a cinnamon roll. I know they aren't the healthiest choices, but she starts school tomorrow and I took her to the mall to buy her some new clothes. You might think it's odd I'm putting her in school two weeks before Christmas break, but I wanted her to meet other kids before—"

He cut her off. "Hold up. Does she have a fever?"

Keely blew out a loud hiss. "I checked it right

before I called Ryder's cell phone. The thermometer said 99.7 degrees. Can you…Ethan, please, can you come over and look at Felicity?"

"On my way." He hung up the phone and headed for the mudroom just off the kitchen.

Baloo trotted past him and took up position at the back door, a hopeful expression in his coal-black eyes. Normally, Ethan would indulge the dog. He and the black Lab had been through a lot of hard times since Ethan rescued the animal during his tour in Afghanistan.

"Sorry, buddy, you can't come with me."

Baloo whined, the sound pitiful and well honed from years of conning Ethan.

"Hang tight, old boy. This shouldn't take long." Ethan scrubbed the animal's face between his hands. "I'll let you out when I get back."

The dog's ears drooped, but he obediently lowered himself to his haunches and rested his chin on his paws.

Ethan grabbed his coat and trod through the three inches of snow that had fallen throughout the day. He didn't have far to go. The backyard of Keely's childhood home spilled into his. They had that in common, both living in the houses they'd grown up in, having inherited them from their parents. Ethan, after his had died. Keely, after hers had moved to Arizona.

He was on her back stoop, stomping snow off

his boots, when the door flung open. "What took you so long?"

Since she sounded like a terrified new parent, he forgave her for her rudeness. "Came as fast as I could."

"Don't just stand there. Come inside."

Holding his tongue, again, he climbed the steps. As was becoming a habit whenever they were up close and personal, he reminded himself this was Keely. Once upon a time she'd been just another skinny kid hanging out with his younger sister.

Despite growing into a beautiful woman with long, gorgeous red hair, amazing green eyes and a figure that jealous peers had once compared to Jessica Rabbit's, Keely was still that same annoying girl Ethan tolerated because she was his sister's BFF.

Except, lately, things had changed between them. Their relationship was morphing into something new, something charged with tension and awkward pauses. The initial shift had started nearly a year ago, right after she'd left her big-city life in New York and settled back in Colorado.

Ethan moved deeper in the house.

The inevitable kick in his gut came right on schedule, as it always did whenever his gaze locked with Keely's. Tonight, the sensation hit him hard. It wasn't an altogether awful feeling, kind of reminded him of danger-induced adrenaline.

Precarious territory. "Where's the patient?"

"Her name is Felicity."

"Right." Ethan shed his coat, tossed it on a nearby bench. "Where is she?"

"Upstairs in her room."

Ethan recognized the panic in Keely's voice, which was mirrored in her wide, almond-shaped green eyes. Her long, wavy hair was also disheveled, as if she'd dragged both hands through the now tangled strands more than a few times.

At the obvious signs of her distress, everything in him softened. He gently touched her sleeve. "I'm here, Keely. I'll take care of the child."

She drew in a few unsteady breaths, her legendary hostility toward him diminishing with each exhale. "I... I believe you."

He dropped his hand. "One last question before I have a look at her. How old is she?"

"She turned seven last month."

His throat squeezed shut. His eyes began to burn.

What were the odds? He swallowed, hard. He'd barely regained his equilibrium when Keely took off at a clipped pace.

Ethan followed after her. They moved at the speed of light from kitchen to living room to stairwell. The smells of home filled him, a mixture of floral scents, furniture polish and freshly baked bread.

He hadn't been inside this house in years. Like a

good neighbor, he'd left Keely alone. She'd done the same for him, a situation that worked for them both.

But now, as he followed her through the house, Ethan wondered why he'd kept his distance. He liked the grown-up Keely, sometimes, when she wasn't being snarky or unnecessarily antagonistic. A couple of unfortunate incidents from the past didn't mean they couldn't find a happy rhythm going into the future. Maybe they could even be friends. Now that she was twenty-nine and he thirty-four, their five-year age gap didn't seem so large.

At the top of the stairs, she stopped outside the second room on her right. Hand on the doorknob, she swung her gaze to his. *Slam*. He told himself he was imagining the body blow. But, of course, he wasn't.

"Keely, after I'm through examining the child I'd like the two of us to—"

A little girl's whimper cut off the rest of his words. Ethan's pulse picked up speed. Blood rushed in his ears. Memories yanked at him, emptying his mind of everything but a miserable sense of grief and loss.

He hadn't expected this strong reaction. He saw kids every day at the office. No problem. Yet here he was, his heart pounding and his breath speeding up. He fought the urge to close his eyes. If he did, he'd be back at Fort Bragg, back to the time when he thought he would be a husband and a father.

A split-second swerve to miss a skunk had taken away that future.

This wasn't about him.

Mouth grim, he shoved aside the unwanted memories and walked into the room.

Keely couldn't figure out why Ethan's shoulders were bunched as he made his way toward Felicity's bed, or why he seemed overly tense. She'd take his behavior personally, but now that she thought about it, she realized he'd been relatively relaxed when he first entered through the back door. He'd only grown silent and progressively distant as she'd guided him through the house.

A tall, broad-shouldered man, he moved toward Felicity at the slow, steady pace of a graceful jungle cat. With his glossy black hair and pale blue eyes, Ethan Scott was entirely too good-looking for his own good. The two days' worth of scruff on his well-defined, square jaw gave him a dangerous edge.

Keely had no problem imagining him in the Army Ranger uniform he'd once worn. She shook away the thought, and lifted up a silent prayer that Ethan proved to be the capable doctor everyone in their small town of Village Green, Colorado, claimed he was.

With heavy, lumbering steps, Keely joined him beside Felicity's bed. Tonight he looked more like a regular guy than a former soldier turned successful doctor. He wore faded jeans and a long-sleeve T-shirt that read Of Course I Don't Look Busy. I Did It Right the First Time.

Typical Ethan, the big, bad, frustrating bane of her existence.

"You must be Felicity," he said to the little girl in a low, rough voice that sounded slightly tortured. What was up with that? "I'm your neighbor Ethan. I'm also a doctor."

In her unnaturally pale face, Felicity's big blue eyes rounded. "You don't look like a doctor."

"That's because I keep my white coat at the office." He drew in an audible breath, then carefully sat on the edge of the bed, his eyes running over the child, gauging, measuring. "I understand you're not feeling well."

Felicity's blond curls bobbed up and down. "My tummy hurts real bad."

"Can you tell me where it hurts?"

She whimpered. "Everywhere."

He went still for a beat, his expression bland, giving nothing away. Keely had no idea what was in his head, but she knew what was in hers. Concern for the little girl she'd agreed to take into her home. The transition from carefree single woman to legal guardian of a seven-year-old had begun months ago, only becoming official this week. She was still reeling.

"Okay, Felicity, I'm going to—"

"You can call me Flicka." Cheeks bright pink,

the little girl lifted a skinny shoulder. "But only if you want to."

The easy, affectionate smile Ethan gave the child was very different from the tight, barely tolerant ones Keely received.

"Okay, Flicka, I'm going to perform a few tests. When I press on your stomach, I need you tell me if it hurts."

The little girl nodded again. There was nothing but trust in her eyes, even while her hands clenched around the bedcovers as if she were preparing to embark on a wild amusement park ride.

Incredibly gentle, Ethan pressed on her stomach. "Any pain?"

"Nope." Felicity's death grip released, as did Keely's fear. But when Ethan moved his hands to the lower right portion of Felicity's abdomen, Keely's breath caught in her lungs.

"How about now?" he asked. "Does it hurt when I press here?"

"Not really."

"You're doing great, Flicka. Just a little bit longer and we'll be through." Ethan continued the rest of the exam with a firm but gentle manner.

When he held Felicity's ankle with one hand and her knee with the other, then rotated her hip, the little girl simply watched him in silent fascination. No gasp of pain. No clenched fists in the comforter.

Keely nearly cried in relief.

Eventually, Ethan stood, said goodbye to Felicity, then motioned for Keely to follow him into the hallway.

The moment they were alone, she asked the question burning in her mind. "Is it her appendix?"

"Nothing indicates that particular diagnosis."

What kind of cryptic, unhelpful answer was that? "Are you certain?"

"She's not experiencing swelling in the abdomen or pain in the lower right region. At this point I don't believe an ultrasound or additional lab work is necessary."

He'd pitched his voice low, as if to calm her fears. Keely wasn't appeased. "If it's not her appendix, then what's wrong with her?"

"She has a stomachache."

His matter-of-fact tone increased her distress. "Is there something you can give her to make her feel better?"

"For now, there's nothing to do but continue supportive measures. Keep her hydrated and resting. If the symptoms persist or worsen, call me and I'll come back over."

Why was he so calm? Didn't he understand how worried she was? "I can't bear seeing her in pain."

"Keely, relax. Flicka has a stomachache, probably brought on by stress or the consumption of junk food or both."

"You're saying this is my fault because I let her eat junk food."

"That's not what I'm saying. Kids suffer stomachaches all the time. I'm confident she's going to be okay."

Why didn't she feel better? Why this terrible spasm of guilt in the center of her heart? "I feel so helpless."

"You did the right thing calling me."

Actually, she'd called Ryder. Ethan's younger brother by two years was so much easier to take. Though he was just as good-looking as Ethan, nearly identical actually, with Ryder there was none of the friction and hostility she experienced in the company of this particular Dr. Scott.

"I mean it, Keely. You can call me anytime, no matter how late."

She gaped at him. "Why are you being so nice to me?"

"Because I'm a nice guy." The grin he flashed her was full of the teenage boy she remembered, the one she'd spun a few girlhood dreams around, not the one who'd humiliated her in front of his friends, twice.

"Seriously, why?"

"I'm giving you a pass because you're new to this parenting thing." His eyes sparked with genuine compassion.

No fair. The man had amazing eyes, long-lashed and full of secrets. She saw sorrow there as well, more prominent than usual.

It wasn't the first time she'd noticed that look in

Ethan's eyes. Their paths crossed a lot, primarily because he often came into her restaurant, Senor O'Toole's, on his lunch break.

He might be the big, bad, frustrating bane of her existence. But the lone wolf image didn't ring true, not tonight. Hardly ever, if she was being honest with herself. The raw vulnerability simmering under that tough exterior made Keely want to reach up and smooth away his pain.

She resisted. "Felicity's really going to be all right?"

"For now." He looked about to say more. He even opened his mouth, but then closed it and headed down the stairs.

Keely hurried after him, catching up just as he was shoving his arms through the sleeves of his coat.

He reached for the doorknob, then paused. "Call me," he said. "Anytime, for any reason."

There were so many ways to take that suggestion, even more ways to respond. She chose the most sincere. "I will, and thank you for coming over so quickly. I really appreciate your help tonight."

"You're welcome." He gave her a warm smile.

Her heart stuttered. It *actually* stuttered.

"Good night, Keely."

"Night, Ethan."

Still smiling, he swung open the door. And disappeared into the night.

Chapter Two

Keely waited until Ethan was out of sight before she shut her back door. The rhythmic sound of the dishwasher sloshing through the rinse cycle accompanied her return journey through the kitchen and then into the living room.

Now that her initial fear for Felicity's well-being was put to rest, Keely's mind wanted to linger on the man who'd eased her worries. She'd hardly recognized her neighbor.

Ethan had instilled a sense of calm. He'd been unspeakably gentle with Felicity and Keely was grateful for that. But now she was left feeling confused and edgy and not quite herself.

With his quicksilver smile and excellent bedside manner, Ethan had prodded awake the loneliness she kept stuffed behind a healthy dose of busyness. She'd always thrived on filling her days with activity, to the point of barely having a free moment to herself. Better to be busy than to open herself to ridicule or, even worse, another heartbreak.

At some point in the past year since her broken engagement to William Cutter Sloan III, Keely had convinced herself that activity helped heal her pain, making her feel vital, needed, wanted even. In reality, she'd been sleepwalking through life, burying her pain and humiliation in work, work and more work.

Well, she was wide-awake now, thanks to the seven-year-old little girl she'd taken into her home.

A sense of purpose swelled as Keely mounted the stairs. She was determined to raise the child to the best of her ability. The days ahead would require faith, hope and love.

It all started with love, as her pastor often said. Keely now understood exactly what he meant.

She paused outside Felicity's bedroom and drew in several tight breaths. Ethan claimed the little girl's stomachache wasn't serious. Keely hoped his diagnosis proved accurate.

She'd never forgive herself if something happened to her cousin's daughter. Keely had promised Juliette she'd take care of Felicity until she was once again free to do so herself.

Who knew when that would be? Six years, nine, the full twelve? It was up to the Colorado Department of Corrections and contingent on Juliette's good behavior.

For a brief second, Keely stood rooted to the spot

by a deep, painful ache in her chest. Her cousin had made a terrible mistake. She deserved forgiveness. Yet Keely couldn't help wondering why Juliette hadn't come to her for help, or gone to any of their other family members. Including Keely's twin brother, Beau, who was dripping in money from his days as a world-class professional skier.

By letting pride rule her actions, her cousin had not only lost her freedom. She'd lost the chance to raise her daughter. As a result, Keely would be responsible for Felicity during the child's most formative years.

Lord, help me to be a good influence. Give me the wisdom to guide Felicity from child to young adult.

Releasing a sigh, Keely took one last deep breath and entered the bedroom.

Felicity lay resting on her side, eyes shut, her hands clasped together beneath her chin. She looked so sweet, so innocent. Keely had to swallow several times to release the lump lodged in her throat.

Nothing had prepared her for this melting of her heart, this wondrous, piercing mix of fear, resolve and deep devotion for a child she'd only met three times before Saturday. She hadn't expected to care this much, this fast. Maybe she was capable of loving again after all. For the past year, she'd wondered.

As if Felicity sensed her presence, her eyes slowly blinked open.

"Hey, kiddo." Pasting on a smile, Keely moved deeper in the room. "How are you feeling?"

"Better, I guess." The words came out raspy. "I'm thirsty."

"I bet you are." Keely sat on the edge of the bed and retrieved the cup of water she'd brought to her little cousin earlier. With her free hand she helped the girl sit up and take a few sips.

When she'd had enough, Felicity collapsed back on the bed with a sigh.

Letting out her own whoosh of air, Keely set the cup aside and brushed back a tangle of blond hair from the pretty face that was a tiny copy of her mother's. "Here's hoping by tomorrow you'll be good as new."

"I don't think I'll be better by morning." Felicity stared at Keely in open terror. "I mean, you know, not completely. Not good enough to go to school."

Keely bit her lower lip. Ethan had been right. Felicity's stomachache had been brought on by stress or, more specifically, by worry over starting another school, her third in the same number of months.

Poor kid. She'd experienced a lot of upheaval since her mother was caught embezzling money from her employer. Sent to live with her grandmother during the trial, then with Keely once the verdict was carried out and the paperwork for legal guardianship was complete, Felicity had undergone too much inconsistency in her young life. A little coddling was in order.

"I've been thinking about that." Keely cleared her suddenly thick throat. "It's late and you haven't had much sleep. Let's push your start date back a few days."

"You really mean it? I don't have to go to school tomorrow?"

"No school tomorrow."

Felicity's entire face lit up, her O'Toole heritage already evident in her pretty, petite features. According to family lore, their ancestors had been world-famous Shakespearean actors known for their extraordinary beauty and charm as much as their talent.

Keely hadn't caught the acting bug, but she'd traded on her looks for about a second and a half when she first arrived in New York City right out of high school. It had taken all of three weeks to realize her talents were better suited for the business office of the modeling agency, rather than the runway.

She'd really loved her job as a booking agent but was happy to be home after a ten-year absence. She had her brother here in Village Green. Her lifelong best friend Olivia Scott, now Olivia Mitchell, also lived in town, and Keely had a little girl right here in her home, depending on her.

"Keely?"

"Hmm?"

A moment of silence passed, and then came a very small, very sad sigh. "Do you think my mom misses me?"

Even knowing this conversation was coming, Keely still felt a pang of dread. What if her words instilled fear rather than calm? "Of course she misses you."

"Do you think she's lonely without me?"

"Your mother loves you," Keely said truthfully, if somewhat evasively. "We'll visit her next month. In the meantime you can write to her."

Although Juliette would eventually be able to see her daughter weekly, she wasn't allowed visitations during the first month of her incarceration.

The holiday season was going to be difficult for Felicity. Since her father had signed over custody before her birth, Juliette was the only parent the child had ever known. Keely was determined to give her sweet cousin the best Christmas of her life. It wouldn't take away Felicity's pain or sense of loss, but it would certainly offer her a lovely distraction.

"I know having your mom gone is really hard, but I'm here for you now, and always."

Choking out a sob, Felicity flung herself into Keely's arms.

With a fierceness that grabbed her by the throat, she pulled the child close and once again silently promised to make this Christmas season one the girl would remember for years to come. "Oh, sweetie, I'm going to take really good care of you, I promise."

Felicity clung for several, long seconds. Keely gently rocked the child back and forth. Once she felt Felicity relax, she eased her back onto the bed. It was hard not to look at her without seeing Juliette. Mother and daughter had the same cornflower-blue eyes, attractive dimples and exotic tilt to their features.

"Will you read to me before I go to sleep?"

"I would love that." Keely sorted through the stack of books she'd placed on the bedside table this afternoon.

"Do we want one of the American Girls, or should I read from—" she picked up the book at the bottom of the pile "—*My Friend Flicka*?"

Keely couldn't help smiling as one of the mysteries from earlier in the evening was now solved. *You can call me Flicka*, Felicity had told Ethan.

Her dimples flashing prettily, the child pointed to the book in Keely's hand. "That one, please."

"*My Friend Flicka* it is." Still smiling, Keely opened the book and began reading about a boy and his horse. Her mind was only partly on the words, mostly on Felicity.

She was a sweet child with an inherently kind nature. Not too many years in the future, she would steal young boys' hearts without even trying. Keely only hoped Felicity's life took a happier route than Juliette's.

Now that she was Felicity's legal guardian, Keely would ensure that her little cousin made wise choices. Keely would start the process by loving her, and creating a stable home and, of course, raising her in the church. *Train up a child in the way he should go: and when he is old, he will not depart from it.*

With the verse from Proverbs convicting her, she turned the page and continued reading. By the time she made it to the end of the first chapter, Felicity was sound asleep.

Keely spent the rest of the night on the phone clearing her calendar and ensuring that her managers were okay running the restaurant a few more days without her. Then she texted her brother and asked him to check in periodically during the afternoon and evening shifts. With his ski shop, the Slippery Slope, next door to the restaurant, it shouldn't be a problem.

The next morning, Keely woke feeling better about her role as a surrogate mother to her cousin's daughter. Maybe, just maybe, she'd get it right with Felicity.

Please, Lord, let it be so.

Just after sunrise, the child herself came into the kitchen when Keely was sipping her first cup of coffee for the day.

"Hey there." She set her steaming mug on the counter. "I was just about to run upstairs and check on you."

Rubbing at her eyes, Felicity smiled around a jaw-cracking yawn. "I'm hungry."

Which answered Keely's next question. Obviously, the child was feeling better this morning. "How do pancakes sound?"

"Yummy."

While Keely mixed up the batter, she and Felicity discussed their favorite foods, which led to the popular chocolate-versus-vanilla debate. Chocolate won, of course.

She made a mental note to stop by her best friend's brand-new chocolate shop with Felicity in tow. If they went in one afternoon this week, perhaps her cousin could meet Olivia's twin daughters, Megan and Molly, who were Felicity's same age and attended Village Green Elementary. It was an excellent way to help the child make new friends in a safe, comfortable environment.

By the time Keely set a full plate in front of her, she knew she'd made the right decision to keep Felicity home for the day.

She was just about to dig into her own stack of pancakes when a knock sounded on the back door.

Thinking she knew exactly who was standing outside her house, Keely chewed on her bottom lip. She wasn't sure she was ready to face Ethan again, not before she'd consumed at least two more cups of coffee. The animosity between them she could handle. It was familiar, comfortable, but this sudden getting along, even if only for a child's sake? Well, that confused and intimidated her.

Another knock came, louder and more insistent. "Aren't you going to see who it is?"

The question spurred Keely into action. "Be right back."

She felt a catch in her throat when she opened the door to a very different man than the one she'd interacted with last night. He'd ditched the casual T-shirt, jeans and—sadly—the scruff. He now wore a pair of dark blue dress pants and a crisp white button-down. He was also rocking a beat-up leather jacket and aviator sunglasses.

Keely sucked in a breath, wondering why her pulse sped up whenever the man came within five feet of her.

Not much got to her. In truth, very little got to her. But a clean-shaven Ethan Scott decked out in professional attire and really cool shades?

Oh yeah, that got to her.

Ethan removed his sunglasses, only to realize his mistake the moment his unhindered gaze connected with Keely's. He should have called instead of coming over to check on Flicka in person. Too late to change his mind now. He was tethered to the spot by a pair of sea-green eyes.

Why had he never noticed how long and full

Keely's lashes were? How had he missed the flaw-
lessness of her complexion?

He tried to look away. He really tried. But then
the doctor in him took over and he noted the
tiny lines of stress around her mouth, the purple
smudges beneath her eyes.

She'd had a rough night.

"Is Flicka still experiencing stomach pains?"

"No, she's fine. She's—"

"Dr. Ethan, Dr. Ethan, you're here!"

Charmed by the enthusiastic greeting, he peered
around Keely and smiled at the girl. She was
smaller than he'd calculated, skinnier, too, but utterly adorable as she frantically waved a hand over
her head.

"Hey, Flicka."

He'd barely shifted around Keely when the little girl launched herself at him. He caught her and
held her close for one beat, two, then slowly set
her back on her feet and studied her more closely.
"Looks like someone's feeling better."

"I am." She bounced from one foot to the other.
"My tummy doesn't hurt at all, not even a little bit.
Are you here for breakfast? Keely made pancakes
and they're really, really good."

As he sorted through the rapid-fire speech,
Ethan's mind hooked on one word. Pancakes. His
favorite. He shot a questioning glance in Keely's
direction. "Is there enough for me?"

"Sure, why not?" Face as grim as her tone, she headed toward the kitchen without another word.

Hardly a warm invitation. But there was one thing Ethan had learned since Keely moved back to town and took over her family's restaurant: She'd inherited her mother's gift in the kitchen. He'd take whatever she was serving, with whatever prickly attitude she adopted. Her cooking was *that* good.

Flicka took his hand and dragged him deeper into the house. "I didn't think I was ever going to see you again, ever, at least not for a few more days."

He chuckled. "I'm your neighbor. Our paths will cross often, maybe every day."

Keely made a soft sound of protest in her throat, barely audible, but Ethan caught it. "Got a problem with that?"

Her pause told its own story. But then she lifted a careless shoulder that didn't ring true with her tight expression.

"Not at all." She blessed him with a sugary sweet smile. "I enjoy your company, Dr. Scott."

They both knew that wasn't true, but Ethan decided to be an optimist this morning. Maybe he and Keely really could set aside their differences and become friends. Neighbors were supposed to be friendly, weren't they? Wasn't that the same as being friends?

Flicka carried the conversation while Ethan dug

into a large stack of fluffy pancakes. He hadn't shared breakfast with a single mother and her daughter in nearly two years.

Technically, he wasn't doing so now. Flicka wasn't Keely's child. Still, he had to focus on his food, and the girl's excited chatter, rather than the unease he felt. The cozy setting felt too familiar, a taste of the life he'd had and then lost so abruptly. Out of sheer survival, he shut his mind to everything but the plate of food in front of him.

Holding painful memories at bay was hard work. By the time he finished his pancakes he was exhausted. He needed to vacate the premises stat. Unfortunately, he'd only dealt with one of the reasons he'd made the short journey across their adjacent yards. He said goodbye to Flicka, included a promise to stop by soon, then asked Keely to walk him out.

At her challenging stare, he tried not to show his impatience. He wasn't in the mood for one of their legendary arguments this morning. "I have something I need to run by you."

"All right, fine."

Once they were alone on the back stoop, he allowed himself a good long look at his neighbor. What he saw put him immediately on edge. She was especially beautiful in the morning light, her hair several warm shades of red, gold and copper.

She'd tamed the long strands in a sleek ponytail. The simple style highlighted her stunning features. Even with her face free of cosmetics, Ethan could easily picture her on the cover of a fashion magazine.

"What did you want to speak with me about?"

A muscle knotted in his chest at her wary tone. The progress they'd made last night was gone.

"First off," he began as calmly as possible, "I didn't come over to mooch breakfast, although I certainly enjoyed every bite. So, thanks."

"Oh, uh…you're welcome."

Her faltering voice told him he'd caught her off guard, as if she didn't expect a compliment from him, which made Ethan wonder why he didn't do it more often. There were many things he liked about Keely. Her smile, her eyes, her quick wit, her smile, her…

What had he come over for again?

Thankfully, Keely filled the conversational void. "You were right, by the way."

He felt his eyebrows travel toward his hairline. "Although I never tire of hearing that, especially from you, it's so rare. But I'm one step behind. What was I right about?"

She made a face. "Felicity's stomachache. It was definitely brought on by stress. Her recovery started almost immediately after I told her she didn't have to start school today."

The comment brought him to the other reason for his visit.

"I'd like you to bring her into the office for a

complete exam." Last night had been an emergency, but Ethan didn't normally treat patients unless he knew their history. "I assume you have access to her medical records."

She nodded. "The school required them for enrollment."

"Bring them with you to her appointment."

"Okay. Ethan, I…" She hesitated, clearly debating whether to argue the point.

He cut her off before she could begin. They were in his wheelhouse now. "Keely, the child needs a primary care physician."

"You're right, of course." She gave him a firm nod. "I'll call the office later today and make an appointment."

"Good." They were on the same page.

"But I think it would be best if I made it with one of the other doctors in your practice."

"Why not me?"

"I… It's hard to explain."

"Try."

She dropped her gaze and sighed again, softer this time. "I guess it's because we're neighbors. It could get awkward."

Nearly everything about their relationship was awkward. But this wasn't about them. Or was it?

"Is it because of what happened at the Young Professionals mixer last year?"

"Of course not."

The response came too quickly. He lifted a single eyebrow.

"All right, yes," she admitted. "It's *partly* the reason."

Something inside him went ice-cold. "You're still holding that against me?"

Her gaze snapped with familiar annoyance. "You embarrassed me in front of Parker Thorpe and two of his associates."

Of course he'd stepped in. For good reason. "The guy was married."

"And that matters why?"

"Married," he reiterated.

"Parker and I were just talking." She huffed out the words in obvious frustration.

Ethan resisted the urge to hiss out his own frustration. He and Keely had done this dance too many times to count in the past year.

Yet, no matter how he explained his side of the argument, the woman refused to believe he'd actually been looking out for her. At the time of the mixer, she'd been new to town and had no idea what kind of guy Parker really was beneath the dentist-enhanced smile and hundred-dollar haircut.

"Look, I'm not saying the conversation wasn't innocent, at least on your end." He held her stare. "But it wasn't on his."

"You can't possibly know that for certain."

"Parker Thorpe is, was and always will be a player."

"As I recall, you said the same thing about Kenny Noble."

Ethan frowned at the reminder. "Kenny was eighteen. And you were twelve."

"I was thirteen. And, besides, I was just talk ing to him."

"You were still too young to be hanging out with a senior in high school. You were only twelve."

"Thirteen," she corrected again, this time with an exaggerated eye roll. "There was no need to tell him how old I was—"

"I beg to differ."

"—in front of half your stupid football team."

Okay, she had a point there. Ethan ran a hand over his jaw and went on the defense. "I was try ing to protect you, not just from Kenny but from all the guys."

"That's your argument? You were protecting me? By humiliating me in front of your friends?"

That hadn't been his intention. Several of the guys had made derogatory remarks about her curvy figure. Ethan still felt a simmering rage whenever he remembered some of the names they'd called her.

He started to explain himself, again, but she cut him off. "I have to get back inside. Felicity will be wondering where I am."

She turned to go.

"Keely, wait."

She spun back around. "What now?"

"Don't forget to call and set up Flicka's appointment. Make it with me or Connor, it doesn't matter, as long as you—"

He was talking to her back.

"I mean it," he called after her, raising his voice over the wind. "The kid should see a doctor for a complete exam."

She stopped, sighed, slowly nodded. "I'll take care of it today."

Despite her reasonable tone, Ethan sensed she was still upset. And that bothered him. A lot. Keely wasn't a woman who held on to petty grudges. If she was still this twisted up about the past, then he'd clearly hurt her and would have to make it up to her.

If only he knew how.

Chapter Three

The rest of Ethan's morning went about as smoothly as his conversation with Keely. Before he saw his first patient, he had a stack of lab reports to review and phone messages to return, nearly all of which required his immediate attention.

He prioritized. Then took action, tackling the refills from pharmacies first, the more involved problems next. Halfway through dictating a letter on a patient he was referring to a specialist, his computer screen went blank. "Not again."

He pounded at a few keys, only to lose most of the work he'd completed in the past hour. Good times.

Mouth grim, he tried to focus, but an image of breakfast with his neighbors flashed in his mind. He hadn't realized how much he missed being part of a small, happy family.

Logically, he knew he'd been living in limbo too long, running in place, moving neither forward nor backward. He wasn't ready for another relationship; perhaps he never would be, but it was time to stop spinning his wheels. Time he got connected in the community and did his part for the town.

Decision made, he opened his email program and fired off a message to a former classmate and the newly elected mayor of Village Green. If there was a volunteer opportunity in need of Ethan's particular skills, Hardy Bennett would hook him up.

Ethan sat back. Why didn't he feel better? Why couldn't he shake the notion that the need for his skills was much closer to home, literally next door? He'd seen something in Flicka's eyes, a sense of loss he recognized on a soul-deep level.

Clearly, the story behind the little girl's arrival in Village Green was an unpleasant tale. Because he knew how it felt to have the future yanked away without warning, the unsettling sensation in his gut dug deeper.

His nurse stuck her head in the office. The Santa hat sitting at a jaunty angle on her head, along with the jingle-bell earrings she wore, was a visible reminder that the Christmas season had officially begun. "Your first patient is here, Dr. Scott."

He glanced at his watch, frowned. Tasha Dupree was ruthless when it came to keeping Ethan and his partners on schedule—one of the many reasons he valued her—but she was way ahead of herself this morning.

"My first patient isn't due until nine." He raised

a hand to keep her from interrupting. "I marked off the extra time this morning to answer phone calls and update patient charts."

"It's a walk-in. And before you tell me to hunt down one of our other doctors, the patient specifically requested you."

Ethan made his way around his desk. Tasha gave him a big, toothy grin. He eyed the nurse more closely. She definitely had an amused look in her dark brown eyes that were the same color as her hair.

Somewhere in her late twenties, Tasha was known for her quirky sense of humor. He had a bad feeling about this walk-in appointment.

"You gonna tell me the name of the patient?"

"I'd rather let you find out for yourself." She handed him the tablet she'd brought with her.

Ethan gave the screen a cursory glance, and groaned when he noted the name of his early-morning walk-in. Lacy Hargrove.

No denying the young divorcee was beautiful. She was also on the prowl for husband number three. Word around town was that she planned to bag herself a doctor this time around. Ethan was currently at the top of her list now that his medical partner Connor Mitchell was newly married to Ethan's sister, Olivia.

Tasha gave him a sympathetic pat on the arm. "Want me to join you in the exam room?"

"Does a chicken have wings?"

The question earned him a dry laugh. "Of all the birds you could have referenced, I find it interesting you chose a chicken."

Ignoring the wisecrack, Ethan scanned Lacy's complaint. When his eyes landed on a familiar word—*stomachache*—his mind went to last night's patient.

Ethan liked Flicka. But she reminded him of the little girl he'd thought would become his stepdaughter. Samantha had been just as sweet, just as charming. With his mind poised between past and present, he experienced a moment of utter grief before tucking away the emotion and focusing on work.

Blinking the screen back into focus, he finished reviewing the notes on Lacy's ailment. Mouth pressed in a flat line, he handed the tablet back to Tasha and spoke in an even tone. "Where did you put the patient?"

"Exam room 3."

"Let's go."

"Right behind you." Adopting his same professional manner, Tasha followed him down the hallway in relative silence, if he didn't count the tinkling jingle bells.

After determining that Lacy's stomachache was simply indigestion, Ethan gave her the name of a good antacid, bolted from the room and continued seeing patients throughout the day.

By half past six, he was back at his desk, staring

at his computer without really seeing the screen. He'd been feeling off since last night's unplanned house call. The encounter with Keely had opened old wounds. This morning's homey breakfast had only made the pain that much more real.

As he leaned back in his chair, Ethan's gaze landed on a photograph from his army days. He was in full battle gear, his arm slung over Tracy's shoulders. He'd been sent to Afghanistan to treat high-value patients. Tracy, an experienced helicopter pilot, had been assigned to fly the injured soldiers in from the battlefield.

It was love at first sight for them both. Following regulation, they'd held off dating until they were back in the United States. Tracy had been a single mother. Her daughter, Samantha, had stolen Ethan's heart nearly as quickly as her mother had.

He'd proposed to Tracy six months after their first official date. She'd died three weeks later in a freak accident eerily similar to the crash that had taken his parents.

Samantha's biological father had shown up at the funeral and taken her away immediately following the service. Ethan's heart had been ripped out not once, but twice.

The loss of so many loved ones had left its mark. Life was fragile and could be gone in a blink. Too much pain came with loving and then losing. He would not willingly fall in love again, wouldn't—couldn't—go through another funeral.

Yeah, okay, he knew it was irrational. He loved his siblings, didn't he? He could lose them, just as he had lost all the others. But why cloud the issue with logic, when he was perfectly happy living in the great state of denial?

Ethan didn't blame God for his many losses. That would give the cold, distant deity too much power.

Needing to get away from his maudlin thoughts, he abruptly rose and left the office building. Once he was sitting in his SUV, the engine idling, he checked the time on the dashboard. Ryder would have left already for his shift at the hospital.

Ethan wasn't especially looking forward to going home to an empty house. At least Baloo would be there waiting for him. Man's best friend.

Fifteen minutes after pulling out of the office parking lot, Ethan swung his car onto his street. His neighbors had begun decorating their houses. Lights blinked from roofs. Man-made snowmen, plastic reindeer and Santa sleighs adorned the snow-coated lawns. He'd been dropped in the middle of Christmas Town, USA.

Instead of soothing his dark mood, the decorations reminded him of the family he'd lost, the plans he'd had for the future.

Once he was safely inside his garage, he told himself for the third time—or was it the fourth?—that he was perfectly fine with Baloo's company for the evening. He actually preferred to be home alone with his dog most nights. He couldn't experience any more grief if he didn't let any more people into his heart. He had his siblings. They were enough.

He could practically hear his mother sighing in disappointment, and Tracy telling him that was no way to live. Yeah, well, they'd both left him. Not by choice, but he felt the hole in his heart, and his life, anyway.

Baloo greeted him with a series of exuberant barks.

Ethan scratched the animal behind the ears. "Bet you're ready to go outside."

Rising to his full height, Ethan glanced briefly out the window and noticed Keely's house ablaze in light.

His throat cinched up tight. Since when did his neighbor turn on all her lights? Maybe Flicka was sick again. Or was she afraid of the dark? The thought tugged at the part of him that had nearly become a father.

There was something about the kid, something in her eyes, a lost look that reflected his own pain. He'd sleep easier knowing she was all right.

And while he was checking on the child, he'd point out to Keely—with extreme patience, of course—that she'd forgotten to make the appointment for Flicka's wellness visit. It was the responsible thing to do.

Ethan was nothing if not responsible.

* * *

Because Keely was standing at her kitchen sink, looking out the window while she washed vegetables, she noticed the exact moment Ethan exited his house with a rambunctious Baloo.

Against her better judgment, she allowed herself to observe man and dog. Halfway between their yards, Baloo bounded into a snowdrift, then popped up with a ball in his mouth and white flakes clinging to his black fur. Keely could hear Ethan's uninhibited laughter as he brushed off his snow-covered dog.

She never saw this side of him. She couldn't help wondering why. She sensed something tragic had happened to him before he returned to Village Green. There were times when they weren't sniping at each other that she saw the grief in his eyes. Thanks to Cutter, she knew that look of loss well.

Though Keely didn't know any details, she sensed Ethan's heart had been shattered by the loss of a woman.

Had it been a death or a bad breakup?

Either scenario indicated a man unwilling to let go of something, possibly someone, from his past. A good reminder, she told herself, that Ethan wasn't the man for her.

That didn't mean Keely couldn't enjoy watching him now. Riveted by the sight of all that masculine energy unleashed in a game of fetch, she continued to stare.

As if sensing her eyes on him, Ethan paused in the middle of his windup. The smile he shot in her direction reached deep inside her heart and squeezed.

Gasping softly, she moved away from the window and that heart-tugging grin. No doubt about it, she was in serious trouble.

What was it about the man? He was good-looking, and sure, she liked good-looking men. What woman didn't? He was also single, financially stable and a successful doctor.

But she also knew he could be arrogant, bossy and treat a woman—Keely—like a twelve-year-old girl instead of the adult she'd become. Added to her suspicions as to why he didn't date, she knew to keep up her guard.

Minutes later, even prepared for the resounding knock, Keely still had to lock her knees and gulp for air.

Felicity rushed into the kitchen. "I heard a knock at the back door. Do you think it's Dr. Ethan?"

The kid had excellent hearing. Keely filed away that piece of information with everything else she'd discovered about the little girl today. Turned out, Felicity enjoyed dance classes and ice-skating as much as Keely had at her age.

She also disliked playing soccer, tennis and other organized sports. Again, just like Keely.

There was still so much to discover about her cousin. At least she'd made considerable headway today. Unfortunately, whenever the subject of school came up, or Keely broached the possibility of meeting new friends, Felicity's face turned gray and the complaints of not feeling well began.

Keely was concerned there might be a larger problem brewing than the child's simple reluctance to attend a new school and meet other girls her age. *Please, Lord, let this be a normal part of the transition into my home and not a symptom of something bigger.*

A second knock sounded. Felicity gave Keely a look of impatience. "Can I see if it's Dr. Ethan at the door?"

"Go ahead."

The door squeaked on its hinges mere seconds before Ethan's low chuckle rumbled in response to the child's excited hello. Clearly, Felicity wasn't shy around their handsome neighbor. The thought gave Keely hope for the girl's future.

"I brought my dog over to meet you," she heard Ethan say to Felicity. "His name is Baloo."

A series of happy barks mingled with delighted little-girl squeals. "He's so pretty."

"Don't let him hear you say that." Ethan spoke the words in an amused stage whisper. "Baloo's sensitive about his gender."

"Oh, sorry. *He's* so *handsome*," Felicity cooed. "You're a handsome boy, aren't you?"

It wasn't long before the child invited their visitors to come inside the house.

Baloo bounded into the kitchen first, tail wagging fast as a whip. Keely smiled at the handsome black Lab. "Hey, big boy."

All but quivering with excitement, the dog leaped at her. Ethan caught hold of his collar just in time.

"Sit," he ordered.

Baloo whined pitifully but immediately obeyed, then politely offered a paw to Keely.

Charmed, she obliged the dog by giving him a hearty handshake.

"That's so cool," Felicity announced, moving in for a better look. "Can I try?"

"Go for it." Keely stepped aside so the little girl could take her place in front of Baloo.

With the same patience he'd displayed the previous evening, Ethan showed Felicity a series of tricks that Baloo could do. Sit. Shake. Lie down. "Now you try."

"Okay."

Only after Felicity took over issuing the commands did Ethan shift his attention to Keely. *Oh boy.* She blamed the stutter in her pulse on those piercing blue eyes. When Ethan zeroed in on a woman, she knew it, all the way down to her toes.

He'd changed clothes since this morning. The five o'clock shadow provided a dangerous, appealing edge. He wore a different T-shirt, but the slogan was similar to last night's: Here I Am. What Are Your Other Two Wishes?

The man really was annoying. Snorting in exasperation, she lifted her head, found herself caught once again in his gaze. She really wished he'd quit staring at her with...*those eyes*.

"Hey," he said with a knowing smirk.

Unable to speak, she hummed out a quick response.

His smile turned into a muffled chuckle. The slightly condescending sound increased her unease. Then came the familiar frustration. Antagonism was one step away. But giving in to the emotion would be childish.

"I, uh..." Keely grabbed the remaining scraps of her dignity. "I wasn't expecting you to stop over again tonight."

"Came to check on my patient." He broke eye contact—finally—and focused on Felicity.

The little girl was running Baloo through his repertoire of tricks a second time around.

"How you feeling this evening, Flicka?"

"Huh?" Hand wrapped around Baloo's outstretched paw, the little girl looked up. "Oh... I'm good. I didn't have to go to school, so Keely and I spent all day baking cookies and making care packages for the Youth Center's Christmas party."

"Sounds like fun."

"It was super fun. In a few days I have to meet Keely's best friend, Olivia, and her daughters, Megan and Molly." The child's eyebrows pulled together in a worried frown. "They're my age and Keely says they can't wait to meet me."

"If Keely said that, then it's true."

"I guess so." She heaved a sigh, the little-girl worry evident in the sound. "Hey, can I take Baloo into the other room and see if he'll play tug-of-war with a sock?"

Though innocently asked, the question brought a complete change over Ethan. His smile dropped, his shoulders tensed, his gaze went distant. It was as if he'd been transported to another place, at least in his mind, somewhere not altogether pleasant.

He cleared his throat, twice. "It's one of his favorite games, especially with little girls on the other end of the sock."

As the two hurried off, an awkward silence fell over the kitchen. Keely couldn't understand why Ethan's entire demeanor had changed simply because Felicity wanted to play tug-of-war with Baloo. She remembered a similar change in him last night.

In the days leading up to their broken engagement, Cutter had looked much like Ethan now. The memory made her doubly wary of the man standing in her house.

Nevertheless, she couldn't stop herself from worrying about Ethan. *He needs me.* The thought surprised her. Ethan Scott was the most capable man she knew. And the most annoying.

And yet…

She placed her fingertips on his arm. "Are you all right?"

Shrugging away from her touch, he blinked slowly, squared his shoulders and drew in a long breath. Once again he was Mr. Cool, Calm and Casual.

"Something smells good."

Now that they were back to polite small talk, a surge of complicated emotions spread through her. The sense of relief was easy enough to understand. The agitation, not nearly so much.

"I made chicken à l'Orange and baked sweet potatoes. And a healthy salad." *Don't ask him to stay for dinner. Do. Not. Ask.* "You're welcome to eat with Felicity and me. There's plenty."

He looked about to turn down her offer. But suddenly, inexplicably, Keely very much wanted him to stay.

"Consider it payment for not teasing me over how I overreacted last night."

"You didn't overreact."

She frowned. "I thought Felicity had appendicitis."

"Given her symptoms, it was a logical concern."

For the second time in so many days, Keely stared at Ethan as if he were a stranger. In many ways, he was. She felt as if they were meeting for the first time. She decided to pretend the change in their relationship didn't matter. But it did.

And that scared her far more than she was willing to admit. The man had too many secrets, none of which he seemed willing to share with her. *Been there, done that, have the remnants of a broken heart to prove it.*

"While we're on the subject of Flicka." He pointed a finger at Keely. "I noticed you didn't make the appointment yet."

She blinked at him in shock. Ethan was arrogant, and the big, bad, frustrating bane of her existence, but he wasn't a micromanager. His office staff handled scheduling. "How can you possibly know whether or not I made an appointment for her?"

"I checked."

Of course he did.

"It's important, Keely. Flicka needs a primary care physician. Make the appointment."

"Felicity really took to Baloo tonight. What do you think? Should I get her a dog for Christmas? Would it help ease the transition for her?"

"Changing the subject, are we?"

"You better believe it."

He laughed. Despite her irritation at his bossy manner, the deep rumble made her smile in return.

Knowing he was right, again, Keely stopped resisting. "I'll make the appointment tomorrow."

"I'm going to hold you to it."

As if she didn't know that. "You never answered my question. Are you staying for dinner?"

His hesitation returned. But this time it lasted only a few heartbeats. "Yeah, I guess I am."

He looked mildly surprised by his acceptance.

That made two of them.

Felicity's laughter rang out. Keely's throat constricted at the happy sound, so different from the groans of pain last night. In that moment, Keely knew she was in over her head. How was she supposed to parent a child she barely knew?

All the fears she'd held at bay since she'd begun taking over legal guardianship shot to the surface. A gasp of utter panic leaked out of her.

Misinterpreting the sound, Ethan's gaze narrowed over her face. "I don't have to stay for dinner. You can take back the invitation and I won't hold it against you."

"It's not that."

Concern etched across her face. "Then what?"

"I… Oh, Ethan, I want to take good care of Felicity, but what do I know about kids? I spent the last decade working in a world of fashion models."

"Keely, listen to me." The epitome of calm confidence, Ethan took hold of her shoulders and gently turned her to face him. "You're doing a great job so far."

Instead of calming her fears, his unexpected words of praise had the opposite effect. "What if I fail her?"

Hands still on her shoulders, he tweaked her nose in a big brother sort of way. "You're exhausted from last night. Once you get some sleep, everything will look better in the morning."

"You're probably right."

"Of course I'm right. I'm always right."

The arrogant comment did what no kind words could have done. She bristled. Prepared for a fight, she snapped her gaze to his, felt her anger melt at his compassionate smile.

That look had her abandoning her pride and admitting, "I'm really scared."

"It's okay to feel scared. It means you care."

Two nights in a row the man had shown her unspeakable kindness. Defeat settled on her shoulders. Because if history had taught Keely anything, it had taught her that a truce between her and Ethan never lasted.

Chapter Four

Now that the emotion of the moment was over, Keely told herself to step back, take a breath, and put some distance between her and Ethan. Things were changing between them, their relationship morphing into something different.

Step. Back.

Instead of heeding the internal warning, she held her ground, drawing strength from the man's solid presence.

She should probably feel embarrassed for admitting her fears to him, knowing he could use them against her one day. Though he'd never been that small and petty. Argumentative, yes, but never unkind. And so she stayed rooted in the moment.

It felt good, she silently admitted, allowing Ethan's confidence in her abilities to chase away her worry. A sob of gratitude slipped past her lips.

He tugged her into a friendly hug. "That's it. Let it out, sweetheart."

Sweetheart. The endearment spread warmth through her chilled limbs.

"Flicka seems to adore you. That's half the battle in these types of situations."

Drawing on his assurance, Keely stepped out of his embrace. To her horror, a rogue tear escaped. Tenderly, almost affectionately, he wiped her wet cheek with the pad of his thumb.

She could hardly stand his casual show of kindness. Any moment she was going to break down in sobs.

Taking another step back, she searched for another topic. *Think, Keely, think.* "I'm determined to make this Christmas special for Felicity. I plan to pull out all the stops, whatever it takes to make her feel comfortable in her new home."

"Tell me what I can do to help."

His immediate offer of assistance didn't mesh with the Ethan Scott she knew, the man who'd turned avoiding her into an art form. So much had changed in two short days.

As she stared into Ethan's blue eyes, she saw the secrets he kept inside him, remembered the way he kept everyone but his closest family and friends at arm's length.

A timely reminder. Never again would she weave dreams around a man who couldn't be completely open with her. And now that Felicity was in her life, she had to think of her, as well.

Bottom line, falling for Ethan Scott was far too

risky. Even a friendship between them carried complexities she didn't want to explore.

And yet she found herself asking, "You truly want to help me give Felicity a memorable Christmas?"

"Isn't that what I just said?" He sounded more than a little insulted.

And they were back to familiar territory, just as she'd feared their tenuous truce a thing of the past. "Somehow I can't see you trimming a tree, stringing popcorn or pinning up stockings to the mantel."

Instead of his rising to her provocation, a look of sorrow came and went in his eyes. It was the same expression she'd seen right before he stepped into Felicity's room last night. Had he lost someone he cared about, someone he'd done all those things with in the past?

"I was thinking of something more manly," he said, not quite smiling. "You know, like hanging your outdoor lights."

Her twin brother usually did that, but with the Slippery Slope's extended hours during the holidays, Beau's free time was limited. "That would be lovely, Ethan. Thank you for offering."

She'd text Beau the good news later tonight.

"No problem, happy to do it."

As they stared at each other, something quite wonderful passed between them. Keely opened her mouth to say something, but Ethan spoke first. "How does Sunday sound?"

She blinked, trying to picture him on a ladder, hanging Christmas lights. The image was entirely too homey for her peace of mind.

This had to stop, this thinking of Ethan Scott as anything other than a distant acquaintance. Thankfully, she remembered she'd invited him to dinner, which was only half done. "I'll finish up in here while you go see if Felicity and Baloo need anything."

Ethan's features softened into what might be considered affection, with a twinge of amusement around the edges. Somehow, after she'd spilled her guts only moments before, that look was far worse than a sneer.

And then he smiled. "Trying to get rid of me, O'Toole?"

No. *Yes*. "Maybe."

He laughed, a deep, masculine rumble in his chest.

Something actually fluttered in her stomach, and her knees threatened to give out. She frowned at her reaction.

"Right," he said, still laughing. "Off I go."

Keely grimaced after his retreating back, trying feverishly to isolate the exact moment when things had changed between her and Ethan. Long before Felicity had moved into her house.

Forcing her breathing to calm, she gathered all

the ingredients for making a salad. She'd just retrieved her favorite wooden bowl when her cell phone rang.

A quick check of the screen had her wondering why the newly elected mayor of Village Green was calling her. She put the phone up to her ear. "This is Keely O'Toole."

"Keely. Hardy Bennett here. I'm glad I caught you."

Her frown deepened at the overly friendly note in his voice. The man was usually all business when they spoke, which was often, since she was the coordinator of Village Green's annual Christmas parade. "Hardy, what can I do for you?"

"It's what *I* can do for *you*." He laughed at his own joke. "During our previous conversation you hinted that your committee was short on staff."

"Well, yes, we could use at least one more member."

Two would be better, but with the parade only three weeks away, Keely didn't hold out much hope for finding volunteers at this late date. Hardy, proving why he'd won the mayoral election in a landslide, offered up a solution to her dilemma.

"I have an updated list of potential volunteers. I'm shooting an email with the names to you…" She heard the click of computer keys. "*Now.* Once you've reviewed the list, let me know who you'd like to fill the open position."

He spoke as if it was as simple as picking a

name off the list and putting the person in place. "I'll take a look and get back to you in the morning."

"Good enough." Hardy ended the call.

Keely opened the email app on her smartphone and absently thumbed through the potential candidates for the hole in her committee. She'd barely begun when a familiar name popped out at her. She snorted. "Yeah, right."

She moved on. Backed up. Stopped. Considered. *Not him, Keely.*

No, she decided, definitely not him.

She scrolled to the end of the list. Then looked again, drawn once more to the third name from the top.

The sound of purposeful footsteps had her jumping in surprise. She bobbled the phone from one hand to the other, then lost her grip entirely.

With catlike reflexes, Ethan reached out and caught the phone before it hit the floor. He started to hand it over but then glanced at the screen and froze.

"What is my name doing in an email from—" he scrolled to the top of the page "—our illustrious mayor?"

"Apparently, Hardy is under the impression that you're interested in getting involved in the community."

"Well, yeah, I sent him an email just this morning asking him to plug me in somewhere."

Confusion dug across his forehead. "But why is he forwarding my name, and these others, to you?"

"Because I happen to have the perfect volunteer opportunity for your particular skill set."

He shot her a wary glance. "What sort of opportunity?"

"Village Green's annual Christmas parade needs you."

Silence met her words.

"The committee is short at least two members."

More silence.

Keely searched his face, but the man was good at hiding his emotions when he wanted to be. At least he hadn't said no. *Yet.* She gave him her sweetest smile. "Don't you want to give back to your community? Wasn't that the point of your email to Hardy?"

"How much time are we talking about?"

"Just over three weeks."

"Uh-huh." His gaze neutral, he passed the phone back to her. "What would I be doing on this committee, precisely?"

"That would be up to the parade coordinator to decide."

"Who's the coordinator?"

She beamed at him. "Me."

His eyes widened. "So I'd be putting my life in your hands for the next three weeks?"

"A bit of an exaggeration but yes, in a manner of speaking that's precisely what you'd be doing."

He leveled her with a dark look, no doubt meant to intimidate her. The gesture had the opposite effect.

Keely would probably wonder over her nerve for years to come, but in that moment, she couldn't help herself. She moved in close, lifted herself onto her toes and pressed her lips to his ear. "Afraid?"

"Not even a little," he clipped out, sounding as though he was forcing the word past jagged glass.

She'd clearly hit a nerve, which had been her goal. Gloating would be in poor taste. So she stepped back and, deciding to soften her approach, explained that much of the work was already done. "We're just finalizing details at this point."

He appeared to consider her request. That was when Keely knew she had him.

This is crazy, she told herself. She needed to spend less time with Ethan, not more. It wasn't too late to let him off the hook, to let them both off the hook.

Instead she found herself nudging him along. "So, I can count on you?"

He nodded.

Giving him no time to change his mind, she shot out her hand. "Welcome aboard, Dr. Scott. Our first meeting is Wednesday night, seven o'clock sharp."

The following afternoon, Ethan took a break between patients and escaped into his office with the idea of reducing the never-ending stack of un-answered phone messages.

He'd barely read through the first one when his mind wandered back to a single moment from last night. In Keely's kitchen, when she'd asked him to stay for dinner. He hadn't planned on accepting. He still wasn't sure why he'd agreed to stick around.

One moment he was introducing Baloo to Flicka. The next, he'd been transported to another time, another home, another *life*. Every instinct had urged him to grab his dog and bolt, before the memories became unbearable.

And yet he'd accepted her invitation.

Things had gone downhill from there.

Now he was committed to working on the town's annual Christmas parade, in a position that would require him to take orders from Keely. Part of him couldn't imagine a worst-case scenario. Another part actually looked forward to watching the woman in action. Something about Keely intrigued him.

She ran her restaurant with efficiency and poise. Whenever a problem arose, she simply dug in and did what was needed. He was becoming more comfortable around her, thinking of her in familiar terms. Not quite friends, nothing so simple.

Then there was Flicka. She was a sweet kid, yet full of a silent, underlying despair that made him want to erase her pain.

A portion of the ice around his heart chipped away, leaving him feeling raw and vulnerable, missing the family that had been ripped away from him.

He spun his chair around and took in the view of his hometown. Village Green was all dressed up for the holidays, a virtual winter wonderland straight off the front of a Christmas card. Along shoveled walkways, storefronts were decorated with garland and twinkling lights.

The festive decorations did nothing to ease Ethan's gloominess. This would be his second Christmas without Tracy and Samantha. Still wallowing in grief from their sudden deaths, he'd found last Christmas lonely and depressing.

Admittedly, Ethan wasn't as sad this year. Yet he wasn't at peace, either. He couldn't shake the notion that he was at a crossroads in his life. The sensation had been growing over the past few months.

A rustling sound from the doorway had him spinning back around. His medical partner Connor hovered on the threshold of his office, his attention engrossed on the tablet in his hand.

"Got a minute to discuss a patient?"

Ethan checked the watch he'd worn in the military and continued to wear as a symbol of where he'd been and how the past had shaped the man he'd become. "Sure."

His next patient wasn't due for twenty minutes.

"I'll keep it brief." Connor stepped fully into the office, then shut the door behind him.

Ethan felt his jaw tighten. He recognized that look on the other man's face. He'd seen it often enough during their long-standing friendship to know whatever Connor had to say, Ethan wasn't going to like it.

He made his way around the desk. Stuffing his hands in his pockets, he leaned back on his heels and waited.

Connor dropped his gaze back to the tablet. Ethan studied his partner's bent head as he punched at the screen. They'd been friends longer than Ethan could remember. They'd played on the same sports teams and run in the same crowd.

But while Ethan had alternated between keeping his siblings out of trouble, working two jobs and earning his college degree before joining the military, Connor had taken the traditional route of college, medical school and marriage to his childhood sweetheart. Sheila's death had hit Connor hard, leaving him to raise his twin daughters on his own, until he'd found happiness a second time around with Ethan's sister, Olivia.

Throughout the years, even with time and distance between them, Connor and Ethan's friendship had remained strong.

When Connor became a widower, Ethan had been there for him. After Tracy's accident, Connor had given Ethan a reason to come home, by selling him half of his already thriving medical practice.

At last, the other doctor lifted his head. "I saw a new patient this afternoon. Felicity O'Toole."

Ethan's heart thumped extra hard as two simultaneous emotions moved through him. Relief that Keely had brought Flicka into the office. And insult that she'd made the appointment with Connor and not him.

With Connor being the father of twin daughters Flicka's age, it made sense Keely would want him to be the child's primary care physician. Nevertheless, if Ethan had any doubt as to whether the woman still held the past against him, he now knew she did.

He was suddenly regretting his agreement to work on the parade with her. If she wanted to, she could make his life difficult, or at least uncomfortable. Except Keely was never spiteful and he'd given his word.

Surely the next three weeks wouldn't be too terrible.

"Keely specifically requested that I let you know she'd followed through her with her promise." Connor shifted his stance, angled his head at a curious tilt. "Want to tell me what that means?"

Ethan gave his partner a brief explanation of Sunday night's events, then finished with "I insisted she bring the child to the office for a complete exam."

"All of which she told me. And yet she made the appointment with me instead of you?" Connor's eyes filled with bafflement. "Why do you think she did that?"

"No idea." Hearing his own heartbeat pounding in his ears, Ethan drew in a tight, audible breath. "Maybe you should have asked Keely."

"I did. She got all nervous and tongue-tied. What *is* it with you two? One would think…"

He fell silent.

"One would think *what*? Spit it out, Connor."

The other man waved away the question. "Not relevant to the conversation."

Since dropping the subject worked for Ethan, he refocused on the practice's newest patient. "Did you discover anything in Flicka's medical history I should know about, in case I have to make another house call?"

Connor's eyebrows pulled together. "Who's Flicka?"

A smile tugged at Ethan's lips. So the kid only wanted him to call her by the nickname. But the warmth that spread through him immediately turned to ice. Only heartache resulted when a guy got too close to a woman with a sweet kid. "I meant Felicity."

"She likes to be called Flicka?"

"Yeah, she does." At least by Ethan.

"I'll make a note of that." Connor typed in the

change. "You can read her chart later, but basically the child is healthy and up to date on all her shots."

Good. That was good.

"She's also extremely fond of you. Throughout the exam, it was Dr. Ethan this and Dr. Ethan that, with a little Baloo thrown in to mix things up."

Ethan chuckled.

"Given everything she's been through," Connor continued, "I suggested Keely create an environment of consistency and—"

"Hold up." Ethan lifted a hand in the air to stop Connor. "What *situation* are you talking about?"

"Keely didn't tell you about the girl's mother?"

"She did not."

And Ethan hadn't asked. *Why* hadn't he asked? Because he hadn't wanted to get too close, or overly involved with the child and her pretty guardian.

No better way to keep things on the surface than by not asking too many personal questions.

"Felicity's mother is Keely's first cousin." Connor went thoughtful again, but only for a moment. "She's in prison serving a twelve-year sentence for embezzlement."

The words echoed in Ethan's head.

Prison. Embezzlement. Not what he'd expected. Even if Flicka's mother served a third of her sentence, and was released on good behavior, she would miss out on a lot of her daughter's life, possibly even the important preteen years.

No wonder Keely was concerned about her role

in the child's life. Ethan's estimation of his neighbor went up five notches. Dangerous ground, since he was perfectly happy keeping the woman at a distance.

"It's been a hard year on the girl. Village Green Elementary will be her third school in as many months."

"That explains the stomachache Sunday night."

Connor nodded. "That would be my diagnosis."

They briefly discussed the rest of the child's medical history. Prior to Sunday night she'd had the usual childhood illnesses, nothing out of the ordinary.

Even though Ethan had access to Flicka's chart, he appreciated Connor giving him the information firsthand. "Thanks for the update."

Connor swung open the door. "No problem."

In the hallway, Ethan fell into step beside his partner. His head was still full of Keely and her little cousin. Now that he understood the situation more clearly, he felt a driving need to make things right between him and his neighbor.

Keely had a challenging road ahead. She would need a friend. Why not Ethan? He could think of a thousand reasons why not. Most of which kept him from making the trek across their backyards later that night.

Chapter Five

Ethan arrived at City Hall ten minutes early. He took a circuitous route to the conference room that led him past Hardy's office—empty, of course—and then to a soda machine that was currently out of his favorite flavor. He told himself he wasn't stalling. He was just killing time.

After a bit of meandering, he located another soda machine at the back of the building. He fed a dollar into the designated slot.

He wasn't stalling, he told himself, even as he popped open the can, and took a long, slow swig. He tossed the can in the recycle bin, then followed the sound of laughing female voices.

At the threshold of the conference room, he looked around and immediately zeroed in on Keely. She was dressed in casual jeans and a green sweater the same color as her amazing eyes. She was setting Flicka up at the end of a long conference table with paper, crayons, kid scissors and several other supplies.

He watched the two interact. They were certainly easy with each other, comfortable even, as if they were already finding their temporary roles as mother and daughter a good fit. The kid's transition wasn't without problems, and could possibly get worse before it got better, but Ethan had no doubt she would settle nicely into her new home. Keely was that determined.

Confirming his suspicion, she said something that made Flicka laugh, which had Keely leaning over and kissing the child's head. There was something unbearably sweet in the gesture and a sense of longing for all he'd lost echoed through him, pressing the air from his lungs.

Ethan tore his gaze away from the charming scene and glanced around the room again. He knew all the people in attendance by name, their various connections to each another and how long they'd lived in Village Green. That was the way of a small town, and why he loved living here, certainly one of the reasons why he'd come home after Tracy's funeral.

It took him a second to realize he was the only man on the committee. Hardy Bennett had some explaining to do. As did Ms. Keely O'Toole.

He moved deeper in the room and was immediately surrounded by seven—he counted—women. Two had been friends of his mother, two were local business owners and the last had sat beside him in high school chemistry.

Flicka came to his rescue, by waving at him and calling him over. With great relief, he said, "Excuse me, ladies, I'm being summoned."

Keely met him halfway across the room. She smiled, soft and sweet, and the expression made him smile in return.

"Ethan, I'm so glad you made it."

"I don't suppose it's too late to back out?" He'd meant it as a joke. But instead of her laughing, Keely's eyes turned serious, even a little desperate.

"Please, please, say you're kidding."

"Of course I'm kidding." He slapped a hand to his heart. "I'm wounded you have to ask."

"Don't tease me like that, okay? I really need your help."

He shouldn't enjoy hearing those words come out of her mouth. But he did, entirely too much.

This was when he usually bit back at her, when he met frustration with frustration, impatience with impatience. But he saw the concern in her eyes and gave her a break. "I made a commitment, Keely. You can count on me to follow through."

She gave a slight wince, so slight that if he hadn't been standing this close he would have missed it. But her expression was full of gratitude.

"Thank you," she whispered, touching his arm to punctuate her point.

He inclined his head. "You're welcome."

"Dr. Ethan, over here," Flicka called out to him.

"Hey." He drew alongside the kid. "What're you doing?"

The girl's eyes sparkled. "I'm making a Christmas card for my mom."

He inspected her handiwork. "Looks like you've got a great start."

"Want to help me?"

"Sure." He settled in beside her. "Better make it an easy task. I have to pay attention to the meeting, too."

"Oh, okay." She thought for a moment, moved around a few items, then pulled out a sheet of Christmas stickers. "You can put these around the border."

"You got it." As soon as he peeled off the first sticker, a sprig of holly and berries, Keely called the meeting to order.

Ethan wasn't surprised she attacked the agenda with the same competence she ran her restaurant. After introductions were made, apparently for Ethan's sake, they hashed out the rules for the parade floats.

Crepe paper, yes; toilet paper, no. Motorized and animal-and man-powered vehicles were allowed, except unicycles because of a disastrous event three years ago. The committee then finalized the list of participants.

Individual reports were next. From where Ethan sat, it seemed most of the work had already been completed and now it was a matter of tackling the various unfinished details. Maybe, just maybe, it wouldn't be so bad working on the parade. It might even be fun. He was so confident of this that when Keely put him in charge of coordinating the parade route, he didn't even flinch.

"No problem." Especially since Keely had already filed the necessary permits with the city.

As the meeting wound down, not only was Ethan comfortable with his agreement to work on the parade, but he was feeling smug.

But then an outrageously late committee member came rushing into the room, a whirlwind of designer clothes, five-inch heels and expensive perfume. To his dismay, it was none other than Lacy Hargrove.

Ethan sank low in his chair, grateful the divorcee hadn't noticed him. Actually, she hadn't bothered looking at any of the committee members. She was too busy discarding her coat and showing off her dress, which was better suited for a gala than a town hall meeting.

Then she dramatically announced, "We have a problem."

Keely eyed Lacy with impatience. "What sort of problem."

"The camels are a no-go."

"Camels?" Ethan blurted out, realizing his mistake a moment too late. All eyes were on him now, most notably Lacy's.

The woman's face split into a wide smile. "I simply can't believe what I'm seeing. You really have joined our little committee."

Ethan boldly held her stare. "I'm looking forward to helping my community."

She started to respond, but Keely cut her off. "Lacy, what do you mean the camels are a no-go?"

"Our supplier has already committed his animals to a neighboring town. I asked him for the number of another traveling zoo, but all the names he gave me don't have camels. We'll have to go with plan B."

Not sure what plan B was, and thinking the lack of camels was a good thing, Ethan quickly scanned the list of parade participants. "I don't see camels mentioned anywhere. Why do we need them?"

The woman on his left answered his question. "To pull Santa's sleigh, of course."

"Why not stick with, I don't know...reindeer?"

Keely shot him a warning look. "You've lived in this town long enough to know it's a Village Green tradition to mix things up when it comes to Santa's sleigh."

"Yeah, okay, but why camels? They're pack animals."

"They don't actually pull the sleigh. It's motorized. We use silk cords to look like reins."

It was good to know no animals would be hurt, but still. "Trust me on this when I say they're a really bad idea."

He knew this from personal experience. Throughout his time in the Middle East, he'd never met a camel that hadn't spit on him.

"We've never had camels before," Alice Wainwright said by way of defense. "It'll raise the bar from last year's zebras."

"Perhaps that's true," he allowed. "But camels are notoriously stubborn and—"

"Ethan." Keely said his name in a clipped, no-nonsense tone. "A quick word in the hallway, please."

Fully prepared to make his case, he followed her out of the room. The sound of chairs scraping against the tile floor told him the rest of the committee had hopped out of their seats, probably hoping to overhear his and Keely's…discussion.

Once they were out in the hallway, Keely spun around, parked her hands on her hips and glared at him. "I don't appreciate you questioning this decision. The committee has already decided this issue by a democratic vote."

"Well, I didn't get a vote or an opportunity to make a case against camels, so I'm making it now. You don't know what you're getting into, Keely. I do."

"The decision is made, Ethan." Scowl firmly in place, she took a step toward him. "Let it go."

He took his own step toward her, going toe-to-toe with the ornery woman. "I've had personal experience with camels. They grumble, bellow and grunt. They're beyond stubborn. They bite. And, Keely." He leaned in so close their noses were practically touching. "They spit."

Holding perfectly still, she refused to back away or give an inch of ground. "You're making at least half of that up."

"I'm telling the truth and I don't appreciate you questioning my integrity."

She glowered harder, but still didn't budge on the issue.

"You're going to regret this decision," he warned. "And I'm going to enjoy saying 'I told you so' the day of the parade."

"This discussion is over. You can either get on board with this or walk away."

The woman made him crazy. Barely an hour earlier she'd told him she needed him. Now she was daring him to leave her in the lurch. "I have half a mind to do just that."

"Don't go." The request came from a small, vulnerable voice. "Please, Dr. Ethan, please don't go."

In a flash, he was on his knees in front of the kid. "Hey, hey, Flicka, there's no need to cry." He wiped her wet cheeks with his thumbs. "I'm not going anywhere."

She sniffled. "But you and Keely were fighting."

"We weren't fighting." Keely joined him on the floor, ran a hand over the little girl's head. "It was just a discussion, but all's well now. Right, Dr. Ethan?"

He tried not to sigh. "Yeah, we're good."

They rose and simultaneously put out a hand to the little girl. Smiling through her tears, she took both and let them lead her back into the room.

How was it, Ethan wondered, that he'd successfully kept his relationship with Keely O'Toole superficial and distant for an entire year, and yet, after a single late-night phone call to help out a sick kid, he was deeply embroiled in her life, and she in his?

A bittersweet pang washed over him. They didn't get along any better than they ever had. But, for the sake of the child clinging to their hands, Ethan promised himself he would try to keep things light and easy between him and Keely. At least, whenever Flicka was with them.

As far as the other times their paths crossed? No problem. He'd simply deal with those on a case-by-case basis.

Keely woke early the next morning to the sound of Felicity crying out her name between loud, gasping sobs. She scrambled out of bed, grabbed her robe and rushed down the hallway in her bare feet.

"I'm here, Felicity." Flinging open the door, she dove into the semi-darkened room, then skidded to a stop at the edge of the bed. Breathing hard, she said again, "I'm here."

The little girl blinked up at her with big, watery

eyes above tearstained cheeks. "I...I...I...had a bad dream."

"Oh, baby." Keely sank on the bed and pulled the child into her arms. "I'm so sorry. You're awake now and I'm here."

She choked on a sob. "I...I think I'm going to be sick."

There wasn't time to get to the bathroom. Keely pulled back, looked frantically around for a towel, but reacted too late.

Felicity got sick across the front of Keely's robe. "Oh, you poor little girl."

"You...you're not mad I threw up on you?"

"Not even a little bit. These things happen."

"I'm really, really sorry."

"Hush now, hush. There's no need to apologize." She paused to wipe a strand of hair off the child's face. "Do you feel better, or do you think you'll be sick again?"

"I... I think I'm better."

"Let me know if that changes." Working quickly, Keely shed her soiled robe and set about cleaning up the rest of the mess. She had to duck into the bathroom for a moment.

Seconds later, she returned with a glass of water and a wet washcloth, which she used to wipe the child's face. Even when she was finished, tears continued leaking out of the big round eyes.

"What's wrong, sweetie? Still upset about your bad dream?"

"No, I…" Felicity whimpered. "I miss my mommy."

Despair pooled in Keely's stomach. For a dangerous second, she was overcome with the magnitude of what she'd undertaken by bringing this child into her home. She knew nothing of parenting, even less of what it took to help a young child feel safe and protected.

"I know you miss your mom, and I'm sure she misses you." Perched on the side of the bed once again, Keely took the glass of water and brought it up to Felicity's lips.

After she took a tentative drink, she rolled stricken eyes up to Keely. "I don't want to forget her."

In that, at least, she could ease the child's mind. "I won't let that happen, I promise. In fact, I'll take you to visit her in a few weeks and then every week after that until she's free to come home."

"I…I think I'm going to be sick again."

Better prepared this time, Keely placed a towel across the child's lap and a small plastic bucket beneath her chin. When she was finished, she collapsed back on her pillow. Her face looked unnaturally pale and her eyes were enormous against her now colorless skin.

Hands trembling, Keely carefully removed the

bucket and towel, then tucked the covers around Felicity's tiny shoulders. In the soft, dawn light her cousin looked incredibly young.

She deserved a *healthy* childhood, deserved a chance to create happy memories that would stay with her forever. Keely wanted to play her part but feared she was already failing.

Reaching down, she swept another lock of hair off the child's forehead. The skin beneath her fingers felt disturbingly hot. Fear replaced every other emotion.

What if Felicity's stomachache was caused by more than simply missing her mother? What if she was really ill? Keely wouldn't be able to live with herself if she didn't find out.

"I'll be right back."

She raced into her bedroom, hurriedly changed into jeans and a sweatshirt, then retrieved her phone. If Ethan refused to help her, and she wouldn't blame him after the way she'd spoken to him last night at the parade meeting, then she'd take Felicity to the ER.

Bottom lip caught between her teeth, she punched out his number. He answered on the first ring, with a curt, "Dr. Scott."

"Ethan, it's me. Keely. I…it's Felicity. She's sick. Her forehead's hot to the touch and she's thrown up twice."

"On my way." He disconnected before she could

thank him, which was just as well. She'd rather do that in person and then apologize for last night. She'd pulled out the *I'm in charge* card, which hadn't gone over well, big shocker.

Hurrying down the stairs, she swung open her back door at the same moment Ethan climbed the final stair. He was already dressed for work in black dress pants and a gray button-down beneath his leather coat.

Thankfully, he didn't waste time with pleasantries. "Any other symptoms I should know about?"

As she led him through the house, she filled him in on the events of the morning. "She woke up about half an hour ago, crying out for me. She'd had a bad dream, got sick, then mentioned missing her mom and got sick again."

They mounted the stairs together, but at the top, Ethan moved in front of Keely and entered Felicity's room ahead of her. His entire demeanor softened. "Hey, Flicka, I hear you're not feeling well again."

The little girl gave a pitiful whimper. "I threw up all over Keely and she didn't get mad or anything."

His response was too low for Keely to hear, but it had Felicity laughing softly and looking less pitiful.

Sitting on the edge of the bed, he went through a similar process as he had Sunday night. But this time he spoke to Felicity about other things besides the tests he was performing on her.

Felicity slowly relaxed and, little by little, her pinched expression released. When the conversation turned to her mother, her lower lip trembled, her face paled, but she didn't cry.

At last, Ethan rose and motioned for Keely to follow him into the hallway. She searched his face, saw a combination of toughness and tenderness that gave her an odd little jolt at the center of her heart.

"It's not her appendix."

The news came as a huge relief. "Okay, good. Any idea what *is* causing her stomachaches?"

"Hard to say, but my guess would be a mix of loneliness and fear, neither unexpected, given her situation."

His words made Keely's throat burn. "I wish I knew how to make things easier for her."

"I've been thinking about that and I have an idea, one you mentioned in passing the other day." His hand closed over hers, squeezed gently. "You can get her a dog. Having a pet to care for will keep her busy and her mind off her worries."

Keely liked the idea, but she wasn't exactly in a position to run out to the pet store this morning and pick one up.

As if he read her mind, a slow, attractive smile spread across his face. "I'll loan you Baloo for the day, as a sort of test run."

Inexpressibly touched, she felt a smile move across her face. "You'd do that for Felicity?"

"And for you, Keely. I'm doing this for you, too."

She felt it again, that jolt in the center of her heart.

It wasn't fair. Just when she was ready to write him off as the frustrating bane of her existence, he did something like this. "When you put it that way, how could I possibly refuse?"

Chapter Six

Later that night, Keely stared at the man standing on her back stoop. He'd changed out of his office clothes and was once again wearing a more casual look, day-old scruff on his jaw included. Thick black lashes framed dazzling blue eyes that sparkled with unexpected warmth.

Not only was Ethan smiling, he'd come bearing gifts from his sister's gourmet chocolate shop, as evidenced by the two bags in his hand. Keely felt herself sigh, which she immediately replaced with suspicion.

What was the man up to now?

Ethan had never given her a gift. Perhaps both bags were for Felicity. Even still, the man standing before her didn't mesh with the man she'd always known, the one who had given her nothing but push back last night at the parade meeting.

"Hey," he said, breaking the lengthy silence.

"Hey, back." *Brilliant response, Keely. That's*

the way to get the man to view you as a smart, savvy woman.

Which wasn't even the point. If she ever dated again, Ethan wasn't the man she would choose. He had secrets that showed in his eyes, right before he put up invisible barriers as thick as the winter coat he wore now. Keely had learned the pain of thinking she could get past those kinds of obstacles. She knew to keep up her guard.

However, after he'd lent Baloo to Felicity for the day, she'd come to the conclusion that she should at least attempt to be friends with the man. They were neighbors. Their paths crossed often, and he'd made two house calls for Felicity.

"You're here to pick up Baloo?"

He nodded. "You gonna invite me in?"

"Of course." She stepped aside to let him pass.

There wasn't a lot of space in the mudroom. While Baloo had slept, Keely had taken Felicity shopping for Christmas decorations. The spoils of their efforts littered most of the floor.

Ethan maneuvered his big, rangy body through the cramped quarters. Twice, he bumped into Keely. Both times, he paused, studied her with a closed expression, then went back to peeling off his coat. His expression held something different tonight, something kinder. Maybe even tender. Who was this man? And what had he done with the Ethan Scott she knew?

He took a step toward her. "Keely."

The way he said her name sent apprehension traveling up her spine. She had no idea what to do with this newer, kinder version of the man. He was being too nice. Too likable.

Unaware of her internal battle, he took her hands. His palms were still warm from the gloves he'd recently removed. "It's long past time I apologized properly."

Apologize? Oh no. He didn't get to take the high road before she could do so herself.

"You made several valid arguments about the camels last night," she admitted, if a bit grudgingly. "And I could have handled the situation with more poise, but the decision has already been made and it's final."

"I'm not talking about the parade meeting. I was speaking about the past, *our* past."

"I...oh."

"I never meant to hurt you, not the time I stepped in with Kenny Nobel when we were kids, or last year with Parker Thorpe. My goal was to protect you."

"I know that, Ethan." She'd been wrong to hold the two incidents against him for so long. "I *know* you meant me no harm."

His lips tilted in a lopsided grin. "So we're good?"

"We're good." She tried to pull free of his grasp. He wouldn't let her go.

"Now that we're friends, would this be a good time to ask you to change your mind about the camels?"

She felt her lips twitch at the hopeful note in his tone. "I never pegged you for a sore loser."

"Who said I lost?" He leaned in close, giving her a whiff of his spicy, masculine scent. "It ain't over till it's over."

"It's over when *I* say it's over."

He heaved an exaggerated sigh. "Seriously, Keely, camels are a bad idea."

"What is it with you and camels?"

"I thought I made myself clear last night. They spit."

Ethan would know, especially after his tour of duty in Afghanistan. Nevertheless, Keely wasn't giving in. She couldn't. "The committee voted. It's a done deal."

"Don't say I didn't warn you."

An odd, silent message spread between them, something complicated and full of meaning she didn't quite understand.

Ever since he'd embarrassed her in front of his high school buddies, Keely had thought of Ethan as arrogant, bossy and close-minded. Her opinion had been confirmed a year ago at the Young Professionals mixer.

But lately, she'd caught glimpses of a different man. Beneath the competent exterior were hints of vulnerability and sadness, the same raw emotions she'd witnessed in Cutter at the end of their relationship.

Wasn't that telling?

Ethan rarely dated, and only for occasions that required him to bring a plus-one. Not for the first time, she wondered if he'd lost someone he loved, a woman perhaps? It would explain a lot. But no one was talking, not Ethan, or his sister, Olivia, who normally told Keely everything.

Whatever haunted the man, it was sad and grave. Her heart softened even more. "It's my turn to give you an apology."

"For…?"

"For wrongfully accusing you of trying to humiliate me. For that I'm truly sorry."

At last, he let go of her hands. "Apology accepted."

Keely was the first to look away, but not before she took a quick head-to-toe assessment.

Ethan looked good tonight. The faded jeans and combat boots were familiar. The T-shirt was new, and read I'm a Bomb Technician. If You See Me Running, Try to Keep Up.

A smile came despite her best efforts to stop it. "Where did you get that?"

"Olivia's Sweet Shoppe." He retrieved the shiny pink and brown bag he'd set on a nearby bench. "Where else would I buy chocolate but from my favorite sister's new store?"

Olivia was his only sister. Still, Ethan's love of

family was unmistakable, and something Keely had always admired about him.

"I meant the T-shirt." She pointed at the black fabric stretched across his muscled chest. "I'm assuming that one's from your days in the army."

He looked down at his shirt. "Probably."

"You don't know?"

He lifted a shoulder. "I can't remember."

Sighing again—why couldn't she stop sighing around the man?—she directed him to follow her into deeper into the house.

"Is Dr. Ethan here?" Felicity's pounding footsteps accompanied the question.

The moment she rounded the corner, Ethan greeted her.

"Dr. Ethan." The little girl practically flew at their neighbor and wrapped her arms around his waist. Before he could do anything but choke out a laugh, she hopped out of his embrace and launched into a detailed account of her day.

When she finally took a breath, Ethan seized the moment to conduct a subtle yet thorough medical exam, mostly questions, then a look at her eyes, ears, nose and throat.

Seemingly satisfied with what he found, or rather didn't find, he presented a bag from Olivia's Sweet Shoppe to the little girl.

And so began another round of hugs. "I love chocolate."

"Who doesn't?"

They eventually moved into the living room and Felicity's chatter wore down. Her energy, however, remained high, as evidenced by the fierce game of tug-of-war she instigated with Baloo and the knotted sock the dog retrieved from beneath a chair.

Keely smiled at their antics, relieved to see the little girl looking so happy, so…normal. The day had started quite differently, all because Keely had introduced the topic of school yet again. If only she could figure out a way to help the child accept new people in her life as she had Ethan.

Give it time, she told herself. But as she watched her cousin looking so happy, Keely decided a dog was definitely in Felicity's future.

Out of the corner of her eye, she saw Ethan watching the two with a sad, nostalgic smile. He blew out a tortured breath, then turned to face Keely.

"For you." He presented another bag from Olivia's store.

"Oh, Ethan, you didn't have to—*oh*." Keely released a soft gasp of pleasure. "You brought me chocolate-covered popcorn."

"Olivia said it's your favorite."

Too choked up to speak, she nodded. *Get control of yourself, Keely O'Toole.*

How could she? She had no idea what to do with this newer Ethan Scott, the one bearing her favorite treat.

"I love you, Baloo." This, from Felicity, as she

flopped down on the floor next to the dog. "So very, very much."

Welcoming the distraction, Keely took in the scene through slightly watery eyes. Felicity and Baloo were both on their backs, breathing hard, staring up at the ceiling.

The sight of them brought back Keely's smile. Expecting to see a similar expression on Ethan's face, she glanced at him.

There was no smile on his face, no tender expression, nothing but an intense look of longing, as if he wanted something so far out of reach he'd lost hope of ever achieving it. Keely had lived in a similar place for months after Cutter withdrew his marriage proposal.

A verse from the book of Proverbs came to mind. *Hope deferred makes the heart sick.*

She desperately wanted to offer Ethan words of comfort, but she didn't know what to say without prying into his past, a past he'd never once shared with her.

"Hey, Dr. Ethan, are you and Baloo staying for the movie?"

"What movie?"

"It's called *Miracle on 34th Street.* Keely says it's a classic." Felicity grinned. "Want to watch it with us?"

"Uh." He cleared his throat. "I—"

"Please say yes. We're making real popcorn, and Keely saved some of the cookies we baked yesterday and…say yes." She placed her hand on his arm. "Say yes, say yes."

Against her better judgment, Keely silently chanted along with the little girl in her head. *Say yes, say yes.*

"Sure, why not?" There was a strained note to his voice, as if it had cost him something very personal to give in to the little girl's request.

"Ethan." Keely touched his arm. "We don't want to impose on your time. Feel free to—"

"I'd like to stay." He gave her a wan smile, the gesture belying his words. "I mean it."

She wanted to believe he was sticking around for all the right reasons. But she just didn't know. She'd called Olivia earlier and gently grilled her friend about Ethan's past. His sister had been surprisingly closed-lipped, only saying that it wasn't her story to tell.

Keely had to trust that Ethan would share his past with her when he was ready, which was probably never.

Some things, she thought with a heavy sigh, never changed.

With only a bowl of popcorn separating them, Ethan lounged on the overstuffed couch beside Keely. What was becoming a startling new habit, he'd accepted an impromptu invitation to stick around with his neighbor and her little girl.

He still wasn't sure why he'd agreed. If pushed

for an explanation, he'd blame it on not wanting to disappoint Flicka.

That had only been one of the reasons.

The other was sitting on the couch beside him.

The more time he spent in Keely's company, the less alone he felt, the less haunted, as if he were slowly waking from a bad dream. Maybe letting down a bit more of his guard wasn't a terrible idea. But if something happened to Keely and Flicka—

He cut off the rest of that thought and hardened his heart. He couldn't—*wouldn't*—suffer another loss. The risk was too high.

He made a point of not looking at Keely, though he was fully aware of her presence. A pleasant feminine scent wafted off her, a girly mix of lavender and orchids. He didn't know what perfume she used, but he'd always liked it.

Breathing in, feeling a bit light-headed, he risked a glance in her direction, thankful her attention was on the screen.

Even in profile, her features were stunning. She had the kind of classic beauty of an actress from the Golden Age of cinema. Rita Hayworth came to mind.

Captivated, Ethan stared, once again feeling something come alive within him. Something he thought he'd buried with Tracy.

He quickly looked away, darted his gaze around the room. The large space, with its comfortable furniture and handcrafted cabinetry, would look good decorated for Christmas.

The season celebrating the birth of the Savior had always been Ethan's favorite. Many of his happiest memories from childhood were from this time of year. He'd wanted to recreate many of his family's traditions with Tracy and Samantha.

God had other plans.

Ethan wasn't really angry at God anymore. But peace still eluded him. Instead of welcoming Christmas with his own family, in his own home, he would spend the day with Olivia, Connor and the twins. It would be nice, but not what Ethan really wanted.

He wanted a family of his own, a wife, children, but he wasn't willing to take the risk of losing them. He shut his eyes against a wave of sorrow, opened them, then zeroed in on a spot at his feet.

Flicka had chosen to view the movie sprawled out on the floor, her head resting lightly on Baloo's back. As he watched his dog so content in the little girl's company, Ethan was dragged back in time, to another living room.

Breath clogged in his throat, Ethan shifted his gaze, this time to a spot on the far wall. He couldn't risk losing himself in memories, most of which he'd tucked away for good. Grief and loss would always be a part of him, but he'd let Tracy and Samantha go. Or had he?

Shouldn't his life look different than it had a year ago?

Keely swiveled her head in his direction. "You say something?"

"Nope."

Her eyebrows lifted. "You were mumbling under your breath."

He forced a smile, grabbed a handful of popcorn, paused before stuffing the kernels in his mouth. "Anyone ever tell you how much you look like the heroine of this movie?"

Keely's eyes widened in disbelief.

"I'm giving you a compliment, Keely. This is the place in the conversation when you say thank you."

"Thank you."

The words came to him inside a soft whisper. He felt a small crack open in his heart, followed by a moment of utter panic. Not Keely. Not her. If he let her in, then lost her, he didn't think he would survive.

"You know, Dr. Scott, you project this carefree image to the world, but I'm not fooled." She poked him in the chest. "You need to learn to lighten up."

"I know how to relax. Just last weekend I went skiing with your brother." Even with his shoulder injury still giving him problems, Beau O'Toole was a force on the slopes. Ethan had been happy just to keep up with the hotshot skier. "The weekend before that I went skydiving with Ryder."

"Oh, well, then, you're not overly intense at all. Don't know where I could have gotten that idea."

Smirking, she returned her attention to the TV screen.

He stuffed popcorn in his mouth, chewed thoughtfully, willing his heart rate to return to normal. Not until the movie credits rolled across the screen did the muscles in his back release.

"Hey, Dr. Ethan." Flicka sat up and rubbed at her eyes. "Can I give Baloo a doggy treat before he has to go to bed?"

Hearing his name, the black Lab lifted his head and gave Ethan a hopeful look. "Sure, but only one."

"Come on, Baloo." Flicka hopped to her feet. "Let's get you a treat before your daddy changes his mind."

The dog dutifully followed her out of the room.

Expecting Keely to follow, Ethan was surprised to find her watching him closely. He held her stare without wavering. Any minute, she would get up and leave the room.

One beat passed, then two, and by the third she blessed him with a slow, sweet smile. His mind went blank, a black void of nothing.

"Thank you, Ethan, thank you for bringing over Baloo this morning. And for working on the parade, even though we both know you don't want to, and for sticking around tonight." Her smile softened, reaching all the way to those remarkable eyes. "Felicity would have been disappointed if you'd said no."

"It was my pleasure." He was shaken to discover he spoke the truth. Nothing much surprised Ethan, or caught him off guard, but everything about tonight had done both.

He was stepping into a minefield of complicated emotions. His heart was thawing, opening up to possibilities he'd hadn't allowed himself to consider for well over a year. The risk was too great, with far too much to lose, maybe more than ever before. The thought made his shoulders bunch.

Flicka's laughter rang out from the kitchen, followed by Baloo's happy bark.

A smile tugged at Ethan's lips, and then moved into his heart, thawing another chunk of ice. "I think my dog is in love."

"Felicity has that way about her."

There was no denying that.

"Oh, Ethan." Her face grew suddenly serious, her expression grave. "I really, really want to do right by this child. But she's not transitioning as well as I'd hoped, as evidenced by her stomachache this morning."

Thinking only of reassuring her, of erasing that worried scowl, he took her hand. "The situation is still new for both of you. You're doing great, Keely, making all the right choices on Flicka's behalf. Like I've said before, consistency and routine will build her confidence. The quicker you can get her on a regular schedule, the better."

A frustrated hiss whooshed out of her. "How can I do that if she refuses to go to school?"

"Give it time, Keely. Do your best and leave the rest—"

"To the Lord."

Not even close. Blind trust had never come easy for Ethan. It had been harder since Tracy's death.

Battling back a bitter response, he forced himself to stay in the moment. It was easier than he would have thought, thanks to a pair of sea-green eyes staring at him with a combination of worry and hope. It was the hope that got to him, the realization that she trusted him enough to seek his advice.

With his free hand, he reached up, brushed a lock of hair off her face, then tucked it behind her ear. Another little-girl giggle had them both jumping.

Keely drew in a shaky breath, let out a tremulous laugh. "Felicity is definitely getting a puppy for Christmas."

Ethan homed in on the change of topic as if it were a suture to a gaping wound. "As I said this morning, it's not a bad idea. Taking care of another living creature will teach her responsibility and help keep her mind off her own problems."

"That's what I discovered today with Baloo. Thanks again, by the way, for loaning him to Felicity."

"I'm sure Baloo enjoyed the company." Uncomfortable with the way she was looking at him, as if he was a superhero, he changed the subject. "So, any ideas about the breed you want to get for Felicity?"

"Not really." A thoughtful expression crossed her pretty features. "I was thinking of getting a dog from the animal shelter."

And there she went again, reaching inside his chest and giving his heart a good, hard tug.

Caught in a haze of admiration, he found himself offering his personal assistance. "Want help picking the dog out?"

"Actually…" She paused. "Yes, I believe I would."

"If we don't have time to speak after the parade meeting tomorrow night, I'll call you in the next few days to set up a time that fits both our schedules."

"Sounds good."

Yeah, it did. A little too good. He was going under, drowning in a deep green sea the color of Keely O'Toole's eyes.

Ethan told himself not to panic. Keely was struggling in her new role as a parent. She needed a friend right now. Once Flicka was more settled, then his neighborly duty would be complete. He could pull away in good conscience.

It was a brilliant strategy for everyone involved. If he stuck to the plan, Ethan told himself, no one would get hurt.

Chapter Seven

Ethan arrived at his second official parade meeting determined to play nice with Keely. Not only because Felicity would be in the room, watching them closely, but also because Keely deserved a break. She'd had a rough couple of weeks and Ethan didn't see the point in adding to her stress.

Now that he knew what he'd gotten himself into, he came more prepared for this meeting than he had been for the last. Laptop in one hand, a to-go mug of strong coffee in the other, he entered the conference room and commandeered the empty seat beside Flicka. "Hey, kid, how you feeling tonight?"

A smile cut across the child's face. "Better. Keely got me this coloring book today and I've been working to get at least ten pictures done before bedtime."

"Nice goal." He'd barely had time to admire the three pages she'd already colored when Keely passed out the evening's agenda and called the meeting to order.

"Lacy isn't coming tonight, but she sent me her report," Keely informed the committee, her mouth thinning as she glanced at her computer screen. "According to her notes, she still can't find any camels and is all out of ideas."

Ethan held back a knowing smirk. As if she could hear his thoughts, Keely looked at him sharply. "You got something to say?"

"That's, uh, too bad?" At her grimace, he added, "Imagine I said that with enthusiasm."

"Yeah, you seem real broken up."

He let his silence be his reply.

Mrs. Colchester, the woman sitting on his left who'd once been his mother's dear friend, tapped him on the shoulder. "Instead of offering platitudes, why don't you fire up that fancy computer of yours and see if you can locate us some camels?"

Before he could respond, the lady on her left leaned forward and gave him a pointed look. "I second that idea."

With a straight face, Keely said, "Couldn't hurt."

"I can help you," Flicka offered, scooting her chair close to his and peering at the computer with wide, eager eyes.

Seeing no easy way out, he said, "Sure, no problem."

While the rest of the committee gave their reports, Ethan halfheartedly surfed around on the internet. Flicka proved incredibly proficient with the search engine, which made her a little too helpful for Ethan's taste. But he was impressed enough not to hinder her efforts.

Keely called for a short break.

Flicka announced she needed to go to the bathroom. One of the other ladies offered to take her, which left Ethan the only one still sitting at the table. Keely came up behind him and glanced over his shoulder. "How's it going?"

Her floral scent had his mood edging into annoyance. "Nothing so far."

"Are you even trying?"

Flicking a cool-eyed glance over his shoulder, he said as calmly as possible, "Yes, Keely, I'm trying."

"I'm delighted to hear that."

She didn't sound delighted. She sounded wary. "Out of curiosity, let's say, I fail to locate camels. What's plan B?"

Her eyebrows knit together. "You don't want to know."

"Oh, but I do."

She closed her eyes and gave a slight, shuddering sigh before opening them again. "Go-karts."

He threw his head back and laughed. "You're actually considering the idea of go-karts pulling Santa's sleigh?"

He was horrified to think she might be serious. "There was a lot of debate, mostly from me, but I was outvoted seven to one." She worked her hands together at her waist. "So now you understand why I'm pushing so hard for the camels."

"I will get you camels. Whatever it takes."

"I think you actually mean that."

"I do."

After a long hesitation, she closed her hand over his shoulder. "You pull this off and I'll owe you one. Any favor, name it and it's yours."

"With that kind of incentive, I better get to work."

Felicity had been in Keely's home nearly two weeks and the girl was still balking at starting a new school. Though she truly sympathized with her cousin's concerns, Keely couldn't coddle Felicity indefinitely. It was time to take action.

One phone call to her best friend and a new plan was set in motion. When she informed Felicity that they were eating breakfast with Ethan's sister and her twin daughters the next day, Felicity had seemed a bit wary, but not altogether resistant.

But now, as they headed into the heart of Village Green, she second-guessed herself. Was she pushing Felicity too hard, too fast?

She would know soon enough.

"Even though I know there's no such thing as Santa, can we put out a plate of cookies anyway?"

Keely squeezed Felicity's hand. "Absolutely. It's an O'Toole tradition. We're going to get a tree, too.

Not a plastic one, either, but a real live one, which is another family tradition."

"Can we take a picture and send it to my mom?"

An invisible fist squeezed the breath out of Keely's lungs. "I think that's a lovely idea."

The poor child had been through a lot of trauma because of Juliette's actions. Keely was even more determined to provide a wonderful Christmas for the girl, with as many family traditions as possible.

"Can we put up stockings for me and you, and maybe Baloo and Dr. Ethan, too?"

"I don't see why not."

Felicity caught her bottom lip between her teeth. "I'd like to hang a stocking for my mom, too, even though she won't be here. And we'll want to put one up for cousin Beau."

"He'd like that."

Although her brother would never admit it, Beau needed family, especially now that his professional career was over. He'd made the most of the situation, by opening his own ski shop and giving lessons to locals, but Keely sensed his restlessness.

Beau clearly missed the life that had been ripped from him after one disastrous training run. He'd been the rising star of winter sports, touted as the David Beckham of downhill skiing.

"Where did you say we're having breakfast?"

"The Turkey Roost."

Felicity wrinkled her nose. "That's a weird name for a restaurant."

Although Keely didn't disagree, she came to the diner's defense. "It's no weirder than the name of my restaurant."

"Senor O'Toole's isn't weird, it's supercool."

Keely's family's restaurant served Irish food with a Mexican flair, a none-too-subtle nod to ancestors on both sides of her family.

With the song "White Christmas" playing on the car radio, Keely pulled her Jeep into an empty parking space and cut the engine. She glanced at the little girl in the seat beside her.

Doubt once again consumed her.

Felicity hadn't complained of a stomachache in days, nor had she thrown up or had any bad dreams. Surely this breakfast with Olivia and the twins would bring the child another step closer to settling into her new life.

"I'm so happy you want to meet Megan and Molly." Keely intentionally put a positive spin on the morning.

Felicity said nothing until they were both out of the car and heading down the sidewalk toward the restaurant. "What if they don't like me?"

Keely didn't immediately try to talk the child out of her fear. She'd spent much of her own childhood feeling shy and awkward. Making friends had been difficult. At thirteen, things had gotten worse when, practically overnight, she'd transformed from a skinny, gawky kid to a fully developed young woman.

"When I spoke with Olivia she assured me the girls are excited to meet you." Smiling to punctuate her point, she pulled Felicity into her arms for a brief hug. "But if you feel uncomfortable, or want to go home, tell me and we'll leave."

"Okay." The little girl visibly relaxed. "While we're in town, do you think we could maybe visit Dr. Ethan at his office?"

And they were back to Felicity's favorite topic.

Though she'd never admit it out loud, Keely shared the little girl's fascination with their handsome neighbor. Now that they were inadvertently spending so much time together, she wondered if they were on the road to becoming friends. *Don't get ahead of yourself, a lot of water under that bridge.*

"I don't know when we'll see him again. Maybe not until the next parade meeting. Dr. Ethan is a very busy man." She said the words as much for herself as the little girl.

The disappointment in the child's eyes mirrored a similar emotion whirling through Keely, an emotion she absolutely refused to acknowledge.

"Come on. Let's go meet some new friends."

The little girl resumed chewing on her bottom lip, even as she heroically lifted her chin and fell into step beside Keely.

A bell attached to the front door announced their arrival. Feet gliding across the checkerboard flooring, Keely took in the 1950s vibe. The yellow Formica tables were paired with pink-and-blue plastic chairs, and the authentic jukebox was playing retro music.

Olivia waved at them from the back of the restaurant. She'd commandeered a large table and had spread out an array of art supplies. Touched by her friend's quick thinking, Keely took Felicity's hand and steered her toward the table.

As they wove their way through the restaurant, Olivia smiled broadly. There was no denying the woman was Ethan's sister. Though her hair was a shade lighter than her brother's, the eyes were the same shape and color, the nose similar, as well. But where Ethan's face was distinctly, undeniably male, and could have been chiseled out of granite, Olivia had softer, rounder, more feminine features.

Glowing with newlywed happiness, she rushed forward and yanked Keely into one of her customary hugs.

"Thanks for doing this, Olivia," she whispered, emotion causing her voice to rasp. "I owe you."

"You owe me nothing. I wouldn't have missed meeting Village Green's newest resident for all the money in the world." Olivia stepped back and smiled at the little girl clinging to Keely now. "You must be Felicity. Come meet my daughters."

On cue, the twins abandoned their art project and rushed over to greet the timid child. "I'm Molly and this is my sister, Megan. We're identical twins."

Felicity looked from one girl to the other, the tension in her shoulders visibly disappearing. "I sort of figured."

"I know, right?" Molly grinned, revealing a missing front tooth. "Kind of hard to miss."

All three girls laughed.

"Do you have any pets?" Megan asked, joining the conversation slower than her sister but with equal enthusiasm.

"No." Felicity shook her head. "But I want one real bad."

"We have a dog." Molly took over the conversation once again. "Hey, Mom, can I have your phone so I can show Felicity pictures of Samson?"

While the three girls huddled over the tiny screen, Keely felt her own shoulders relax. With their blond hair a full shade lighter than Felicity's, the Mitchell twins looked like their father. They had sweet, delicate features and what everyone in town called "Mitchell eyes," an unusual pale amber color that looked like finely spun gold.

Once they showed off their dog, Molly asked Felicity if she wanted to make a holiday box.

"What's that?"

"It's for school. We're going to make greeting cards for everyone in our class and then put them in the boxes during the holiday party."

"You mean like Valentine's Day?"

"Exactly," Molly confirmed. "Mom brought enough supplies for all three of us."

Megan took her hand and pulled her toward the table. "We'll help you get started."

Keely felt her eyes blur with tears of relief. The Mitchell girls were such kind, caring children and Felicity already seemed comfortable around them.

If anyone could understand some of what her cousin was going through, it would be Molly and Megan. They'd lost their mother to cancer when they were four. Connor had done an excellent job raising them on his own. But then Olivia had returned to town and stepped in as a temporary nanny when his housekeeper had busted up her knee.

The two had fallen hopelessly in love within months. Keely didn't begrudge her friend one ounce of the happiness she'd found with Connor. And yet she felt a pang in her heart whenever she was around the newlyweds. Their obvious joy in each other gave Keely a sense of deep, hopeless yearning for something she'd almost had with Cutter—almost, but not quite.

She only wanted a smidge of her friend's happiness. And despite her heartbreak, she still wanted to build a life with a man she loved, who loved her in return. Cutter hadn't been that man. Next time she gave her heart away, she would make sure the man was free to love her.

The tinkling bell attached to the front door heralded a new arrival. Keely glanced over her shoulder and felt her breath catch in her lungs.

She watched Ethan enter the diner with his long-legged, rangy stride. He saw her and smiled. The gesture sent set her heart tripping over itself. Stupid heart.

Chapter Eight

Once a week, Ethan picked up breakfast for his office staff as a thank-you for keeping the practice running smoothly. Six months ago, he'd changed the day to earlier in the week when he discovered his sister and her friends—primarily Keely—met for their scheduled Bible study on Friday morning.

Which raised the question, what were they—*Keely*—doing at the Turkey Roost this morning? Maybe she hadn't noticed him.

Unlikely, since his gaze was locked with hers. He watched, intrigued, as Keely purposely relaxed her stance. He didn't buy the casual pose; too many emotions flitted across her face.

She took a faltering step toward him, then stopped.

His gaze zeroed in on the tiny lines around her mouth, and the purple smudges beneath her eyes. Was Flicka sick again? Or were those signs of stress due to Keely's concerns about her new role in the child's life?

Ethan felt a powerful need to put the woman at ease, to attack her concerns with logic and reason. She'd already proven herself a capable stand-in mother. He had no doubt Flicka was in excellent hands. Still, he sympathized with Keely's worry.

The child was in her care indefinitely, with no real idea when her tenure as guardian would end. That had to weigh heavy on her heart, not knowing when she would have to say goodbye to the child she so clearly loved.

Ethan's gut twisted. He knew the loss she would suffer when that day arrived. His breakfast order forgotten, he headed toward the back of the diner.

A little-girl squeal had his feet grinding to a halt. "Dr. Ethan, Dr. Ethan, you're here. You're really, really here."

Deserting the table and whatever art project she'd been working on, Flicka practically broke out in a run to meet him halfway across the diner.

Her excitement was so genuine his heart slammed against his ribs. "Hey, kiddo."

He barely had time to brace himself before her skinny arms shot out and wrapped around his waist. He had no defense against her uninhibited show of affection. And yet he knew it was a mistake to get too close.

She pulled back and grinned. "I didn't know when I was going to see you again. Keely said it could be days and days."

"She said that, huh?" He shot a glance at the woman in question.

A rush of color hit her cheeks. "You're a busy man."

"Not that busy."

Her only response was a quick shrug.

"Hi, Uncle Ethan."

"Well, well, if it isn't Squirt One." He ruffled Molly's hair, then repeated the process with her sister. "And Squirt Two."

The girls grinned at the nicknames he'd given them long before Olivia married Connor. They were cute kids, sweet, outgoing, and now he understood the reason for this early-morning breakfast. Keely was attempting to introduce Flicka to other children her age, in a neutral setting that would help put her at ease. Clever.

Molly pulled on his sleeve and, with no small amount of pride, said, "We were just showing our new friend pictures of Samson. She thinks he's cute."

"He's *really* cute," Flicka confirmed, an unmistakable look of longing in her eyes.

"Have you met Baloo yet?" Megan asked her.

Felicity gave a fast head bob. "I love Baloo. He can sit and lie down and shake hands and he really likes to play tug-of-war with a sock."

Ethan started to tell Flicka she could play with Baloo again tonight, but Olivia broke into the conversation. "Girls, we need to order breakfast soon, or you'll be late for school."

With the efficiency reminiscent of their mother, Ethan's sister herded all three children back to the table while also motioning for the waitress. He noticed the various supplies on the table and figured one of the women had thought to keep the girls occupied with some sort of art project.

"Want to join us for breakfast?" Olivia asked him.

Tempted, he eyed his sister. He had time, as long as he ate quickly. However, if he knew Keely—which, surprisingly, he was beginning to think he did—he would guess she was helping Flicka make friends. His presence might hinder the process.

His suspicions were confirmed when a silent appeal entered Keely's gaze. Odd that he knew exactly what that look meant.

"Sorry, Liv, can't. Gotta get back to the office."

As if they'd practiced for this moment all morning, the three girls begged him to stay, their voices ringing out in perfect harmony, hitting a high note only Baloo could hear.

"Next time," he promised, touched by the adorable display. He turned to go, then stopped beside Keely. "Got a sec?"

Confusion covered her face, followed immediately by annoyance.

"I'm kind of in the middle of something here."

She looked pointedly look at Felicity. "Can it wait until later?"

Of course, it could wait.

But something in him wouldn't let it go. "I'll be quick."

By the sound she made in her throat, half frustration, half protest, he expected her to refuse. She surprised him by saying, "I'll walk you out."

At the door, he touched her arm. "Hang tight."

He veered back to the cash register, picked up his standing order, then opened the door for Keely to exit ahead of him.

As she moved to a spot beneath the heated awning, Ethan studied her more closely. She wore her red hair in long, soft, curling waves. Her dark-wash jeans looked new, as did the green and gold sweater that highlighted her eyes, simple yet elegant, just like the woman herself.

Ethan realized he'd seen her in a dozen different ways, everything from formal to casual, from runway-ready to sweatpants sloppy.

His gut dipped at the insight that he was this aware of his gorgeous neighbor. What was it about Keely that got to him?

He wanted to say it was tied up in their long, tumultuous history, but that wouldn't be completely accurate. Something new was growing between them, something complex. There was an appealing innocence about Keely O'Toole, a vulnerability that called to the protector in him.

Not that he thought of her as weak. The woman was no pushover, as she'd proven in her role as the parade coordinator. Her inner strength was refreshing.

"You wanted to speak with me?" she asked.

When he didn't respond right away, she smiled the secret smile of woman. That was all it took to scramble his thoughts.

She moved a step closer and suddenly he could smell her shampoo, made from ingredients he couldn't quite pinpoint.

The day he arrived in Afghanistan, his CO had told him he had one job to do, treat the wounded to the best of his ability. Simple instructions, complex task. That was similar to the way he felt around Keely. Simple interactions, complex emotions.

Further complicating matters, she was a mother now, a package deal. If Ethan allowed himself to fall for her, and subsequently for Flicka, he would have to accept that he could lose them, as he had lost so many other people he'd loved. If he kept that salient point in mind, every decision he made concerning Keely and Flicka would be easier.

Her smile turned into a little laugh. "Tick tock, Ethan. I need to get back to Felicity and the girls."

His lips twitched. Bossy, take-charge, snippy Keely was one of his favorites. "I thought we'd set the date to go dog shopping."

"You want to firm up our plans? That's what couldn't wait?"

When she put it that way...

He dug in his heels.

"As you told Flicka, I'm a busy man." He used her own words against her. "If we don't figure out a time soon, we may never coordinate our schedules, and then you could miss out on a really great dog."

Something flashed in her eyes and he suddenly remembered their standoff at that first parade meeting. He'd felt something shift inside him that night, away from hostility toward something far more pleasant. The sensation slammed into him now.

He, Ethan Scott, a man who'd been to war, who'd been twice tasked with burying loved ones, was done in by a pretty scowl. Not on his watch.

"You know I'm right," he said, driving home his point with a challenging grin.

"Let me check my calendar and get back to you later today."

He tapped the tip of her nose. "You do that."

With nothing more to say, he headed down the sidewalk.

Keely's frustrated sigh followed in his wake.

He looked over his shoulder and shot her a wink.

She blushed prettily.

Now, that, he decided, was a fine way to start his day.

At 3:25 p.m., Keely pulled into the carpool line at Village Green Elementary. Her plan to introduce Felicity to the Mitchell twins had proven far more successful than she'd hoped. Her only goal had been to help the little girl make friends, and thereby settle into her home with greater ease.

But once breakfast was finished and it was time for Megan and Molly to head off to school, Felicity had begged to go, too. With the paperwork already complete, it had been a simple matter of checking her in at the office.

As the guidance counselor escorted Felicity to her classroom, the little girl had practically skipped down the hallway. She hadn't looked back at Keely once.

Ethan had been a far different story this morning.

Keely let out a long, exasperated sigh. The wink had been unexpected. Her breath had stalled in her lungs, and all she could do was stand there under the awning, watching him stroll down the street with that ambling, loose-limbed gait.

Any man that good-looking, that strong and capable, should come with a warning label.

The school bell buzzed. Swarms of children soon spilled out of the front door. Keely climbed out of her Jeep and hurried to stand on the sidewalk so Felicity would see her. She'd half expected to get a call from the school nurse, but the child had made it through the entire day. Progress.

Keely waved at Olivia sitting in the carpool line

three cars back, then set her gaze back on the front doors. Any minute now, she would see Felicity.

She exited with several other little girls, the Mitchell twins included. They scattered onto the sidewalk. One by one, each girl sped away from the group toward a waiting car.

Felicity looked around, and then her gaze converged with Keely's. She lifted a hand in greeting.

A smile split across the child's face. She said something to the Mitchell twins and then rushed ahead of them. "I had the best day ever. I can't wait to tell you everything."

"I can't wait to hear everything." Heart full of relief, she opened the door for the girl to scramble into the Jeep.

Keely hadn't even pulled away from the curb before Felicity began regaling her with the events of her day.

"I learned so much. I'm not behind or anything. I think math is going to be my favorite subject." She took a breath. "Oh, and the other kids were really nice to me. Well, except Kale Rivers, but he's mean to everyone." She took another breath. "I love my new teacher, Mrs. Donnelly. She said she was going to call you tonight. I'm not in trouble or anything. She just wants to touch base with you."

Trying desperately to keep up with the child's monologue, Keely took a right turn and caught sight of Felicity's lively face out of the corner of her eye.

There was such joy in her gaze. Keely's stomach fluttered with a mixture of happiness and sorrow. Happiness for all she would share with Felicity, sorrow for Juliette. She would miss so much of her daughter's life. Keely had to swallow several times to dislodge the ache in her throat.

"The best part of the day was recess. Molly and Megan introduced me to their two best friends, Hailey and Brenna. They're my friends now, too."

Oh, thank You, Lord. Perhaps Felicity's transition would be easier than she'd originally thought.

Only as they entered their neighborhood did the child wind down long enough to notice the packages in the back of the Jeep. "Hey, what's in the shopping bags?"

"See for yourself."

Felicity swiveled in her seat to get a better look. "It looks like school supplies and art stuff. Why art stuff?"

"For your holiday box."

Felicity swung back around. "Can we work on it as soon as we get home?"

Home. The word melted Keely's heart into a puddle. Maybe, just maybe, they were past the rough patch.

Thank You, Lord. Thank You for the privilege of caring for this child, no matter how temporary.

"Do you have any other homework?"

"Only the holiday box," Felicity said. "It was due today, but I get extra time because I'm new."

"Then let's get to it as soon as we unpack our supplies."

She hit the button for the garage door and nosed the Jeep forward. After cutting the engine, she grabbed a handful of bags and led the way inside the house. The project was nearly complete when a light snowfall began.

Distracted, Felicity danced to the window. "It's snowing."

"So it is."

The child's voice turned wistful. "I *love* playing in the snow."

Keely did, too. Feeling a surge of excitement, she joined Felicity at the window, took note of the fat flakes clinging to barren tree branches.

"Should we build a snowman?" she asked Felicity.

"Oh, can we?"

The excitement on Felicity's face gave Keely renewed hope they were on the right path. "Absolutely."

They quickly dressed in their coats, hats, scarfs and gloves, then hurried into the backyard, talking and laughing.

Keely tested the snow to make sure it was packable. The tiny clump in her palms was soon perfectly round. With Felicity bouncing on her toes,

Keely kept adding snow until the mound was nearly too big to hold.

"Okay." She set it on the ground. "Help me roll this across the yard."

Felicity moved in next to her. Tongue caught between her teeth, the little girl went to work. Apparently, Keely's cousin took her snowman-building seriously. Another trait they shared.

Felicity rolled while Keely added, packed and molded until the snowball gained a sizable girth. They turned and headed back in the opposite direction just as Ethan's back door creaked. Keely looked up to see Baloo vault out of the house. The excited dog danced in frantic circles around his owner.

Felicity stopped midroll and pointed. "Look. It's Baloo and Dr. Ethan."

At the sound of his name, the dog did two full spins, then sped across the yard, snowflakes flying in his wake. Baloo greeted Felicity with happy barks.

Caught in the sweet moment, Keely laid a hand on her heart. So captured by the scene, she forgot that wherever Baloo went, Ethan soon followed.

She glanced over her shoulder, allowing herself one long look into piercing blue eyes, then felt her own narrow. *Oh no.*

Ethan reached down and scooped up a large handful of snow.

"Don't you dare," Keely warned, hands on hips, scowl firmly in place. "Don't even think about it."

"What?" His grin flashed, quick and devastating. "Can't a guy create a perfectly round masterpiece of snow without someone questioning his motives?"

"I mean it, Ethan. Put down the snowball and walk away."

She spoke a heartbeat too late.

"Consider this payment for conning me into working on the parade with you." Ethan's perfectly round masterpiece sailed in a wide, looping arc.

Keely took off at a dead run, and felt the snowball hit her in the middle of her back.

Sputtering in outrage, she quickly ran for cover. "This means war, Dr. Scott."

Chapter Nine

While Keely hid behind the thick trunk of a cottonwood tree, Ethan packed another snowball with quick, sure hands. Then, when she made the mistake of abandoning cover to issue a series of ridiculous threats, he fired.

It skimmed her right shoulder. She stammered out another warning, but then wisely retreated behind the tree.

"You have no idea who you're up against." The dire threat lost its impact, primarily because it was uttered from behind a tree large enough to hide a small SUV.

Ethan laughed, even as he sent three more snowballs at Keely in rapid-fire succession.

She pelted him with her own arsenal of snowballs. The woman had impressive aim. He dodged to his left, bobbed to the right, but still took one in the chest, another in his left kneecap.

It wasn't until the fight was in full swing that Flicka realized she was missing out on the fun.

Ethan immediately claimed the kid for his team. "You make the snowballs," he said. "I'll throw them."

"Great idea." She dropped to her knees and got to work.

"Hey," Keely called out from behind her tree. "No fair, that's two against one."

"You can have Baloo," he offered, lobbing a slow pitch over the animal's head. The dog caught the snowball midair.

"Gee, thanks, Ethan, how kind of you to even out the odds."

Baloo took another leap, this time catching the snowball Keely fired at Ethan. "I rest my case," she shouted, but he heard the humor in her voice.

Ethan switched jobs with Flicka. After the kid got in a few solid hits, and took one herself, Ethan called a truce.

Keely sauntered out from around her side of the tree. "Giving up already?"

"Brave words from someone covered in snow." He swaggered in her direction, hands out, palms facing her.

Adopting a similar pose, she made her way toward him. When only a few feet separated them, she casually lowered her hands and reached inside her jacket. Smiling sweetly, she lifted herself onto her toes and smashed a handful of snow in his face.

"That's for not fighting fair," she whispered in his ear.

Torn between laughing and revenge, he chose something in between. Roping his arms around her waist, he pulled her flush against him.

"What...what are you doing?"

The words came out a little breathless, egging him on in ways he couldn't begin to describe. "Payback, Keely."

"Ethan, I'm warning you—"

"Yeah, yeah, heard that one before." Blinking snow out of his eyes, he gave Flicka a sidelong glance. "Want to learn how to make a perfect snow angel?"

"I do, I do."

"Your cousin has agreed to demonstrate the proper technique."

Keely gasped. "Ethan, no. Don't. I...I'm..."

"You...you're...what?"

"Cold."

"Nothing like a little physical activity to warm you up. Trust me on this," he whispered in her ear. "I'm a doctor."

Hooking his foot around the back of her knees, he dumped her gently atop the snow-covered ground.

Flat on her back, she glared. "You will pay for this."

The threat was issued as both a challenge and a promise. The woman made him smile.

Hands on hips, he leaned over her. "You're supposed to move your arms up and down, your legs side to side, kind of like jumping jacks on your back."

"I know how to make a snow angel."

Flicka moved in beside him, adding her own words of encouragement. "Come on, Keely, you can do it. Move your arms and legs like Dr. Ethan said."

Lips pressed tightly together, she went through the motions, finishing up by pressing her head back into the snow.

"Well done," Ethan praised, earning him another fierce expression. No doubt about it, Keely O'Toole had a lovely scowl, the kind that made a man stop and take notice.

"You going to stand there grinning at me like a big sap, or help me up?"

He was *really* starting to like this woman.

"Now, pay close attention, Flicka. Making a perfect snow angel is all in the dismount."

Reaching out, he waited for Keely to accept his assistance. She remained unmoving.

He wiggled his fingers.

"Fine." She placed her hands in his, set her heels atop his toes. He yanked her up, catching her against him before her feet touched the ground.

For a dangerous moment, his mind went blank but for the woman in his arms. The world melted away.

"My turn," Flicka declared.

A little mournfully, Ethan set Keely on the ground and then turned to the bouncing child beside him. "Let's find a clean spot in the snow."

Near the property line between the two houses, he dumped the girl gently in the snow, encouraged her to move her arms and legs, then hauled her up.

Back on terra firma, she spun around and studied her snow angel with fierce concentration. "Mine's smaller than Keely's."

"But just as pretty."

"You think so?"

"I know so."

She smiled, her eyes shining from beneath her bright pink ski cap. The child was so sweet, so trusting, so much like another little girl he'd once loved like a daughter. Feeling the pull of memories, Ethan forced himself to stay in the moment.

"Want to help us finish the snowman Keely and I started?"

He pulled in a hard breath. "Sure."

Anything to keep his mind off the past.

Head down, he focused on the mechanics of stacking three snowballs on top of one another, largest to smallest. Keely and Flicka packed snow between the gaps. Baloo offered his assistance by dancing around and eating snow.

"Time to bring the snowman to life." Keely disappeared inside her house and returned with a cowboy hat, a Christmas bandanna, and assorted other items.

They let Flicka do most of the work, and then they all stepped back and admired the finished product. The cowboy hat and bandanna gave the snowman a Western look that somehow worked with the rugged mountains as a backdrop.

"Best snowman ever," Flicka declared, clapping her hands.

Keely met Ethan's gaze. There was something in her smile. Gratitude. Relief. Understanding the sentiment perfectly, he held out his hand for a fist bump, then repeated the process with Flicka. "We make a great team."

"Who wants hot cocoa?" Keely asked.

Ethan wavered between acceptance and retreat. He was already in too deep, grasping for a dream that belonged to his former life, the portion of himself he'd buried with the woman he'd lost on a North Carolina highway.

"We have the tiny marshmallows," Flicka added.

Ethan had no defense against all that little-girl innocence. "Tiny marshmallows are my favorite."

They stomped into Keely's mudroom. Ethan dried off Baloo's paws. Only once he was sure the dog wouldn't track in any unwanted snow or mud did Ethan shed his coat and gloves.

A soft, feminine laugh slipped out of Keely. "Okay, there has to be a story behind that one."

She pointed to his chest when he simply stared at her.

Realizing she meant the slogan on his T-shirt, he

looked down. My Favorite Number of the Alphabet Is Blue.

"Olivia gave this to me on my birthday, something about my mind working differently than most."

"So true."

Keely punctuated the statement with a laugh. The sound had Ethan clearing his throat. "Someone mentioned hot cocoa?"

"Follow me."

He paused on the threshold of the kitchen, took in the table speckled with colorful ribbons, wrapping paper and so many sparkles he thought he might have contracted retina-burn.

"Hate to tell you this, Keely, but, uh…" He blinked. "…a glitter bomb went off in your house."

Her snort of amusement was drowned out by Flicka's excited explanation, something about holiday boxes and handmade Christmas cards. The kid spoke fast, but his mind hooked on one word. "You went to school today? That's awesome."

"I'm in Megan and Molly's class."

"Even better."

"I know." She absently petted the dog glued to her side. "Hey, can I take Baloo in the other room and give him a doggy treat?"

The topic change was so swift, Ethan was pretty sure he had whiplash. He managed a nod.

"Great. Come on, Baloo."

The besotted animal followed after the little

girl. Ethan felt a wave of fondness wash over him. "That's one awesome kid."

"She is, isn't she?" Keely maneuvered in beside him and they stood side by side in companionable silence.

Something almost peaceful filled him. "Did you check your calendar?"

"Why?"

"For our trip to the—" He cut off his own words, craned his head around the doorjamb, then whispered, "Animal shelter."

"You still want to help me pick out a dog for Felicity?"

He couldn't understand why that surprised her, but clearly it did. "Well, yeah."

"I'm only available during a small window Friday morning," she said, not quite meeting his eyes, "after I drop Felicity at school and before the lunch crowd descends on the restaurant."

"Friday morning works for me."

Her gaze whipped to his. "Don't you have to see patients?"

"I'll rearrange a few things."

She continued staring at him, as if she couldn't quite believe he wanted to help her. He hated that she thought so little of him, that he'd given her a reason to distrust his motives in their long, complicated relationship. "So, are we a go?"

"We're a go." It was her turn to clear her throat.

"I'll…uh, make the hot cocoa while you go check on Felicity and Baloo."

"Trying to get rid of me, O'Toole?"

"What? No. What gave you that idea?"

He laughed at her uneasy tone, a deep, low rumble in his chest that felt entirely too good. A surge of guilt reared, as if he was betraying Tracy by having so much fun with Keely.

The sensation was all too familiar. "This is becoming a habit," he muttered.

And he didn't only mean the sense of betrayal, but also his desire to hang out with Keely and Flicka when there was no real reason to do so.

His heart was thawing, as if slowly letting go of the family he'd lost and grasping for the one right in front of him. But with caring came too much risk; with love came pain and grief. As long as he kept things shallow between him and Keely, no one would get hurt.

With that in mind, he stayed only long enough to consume one cup of cocoa, then he made his excuses. Keely didn't try to stop him from leaving. In fact, she'd all but rushed him out the door.

It was a good thing, he told himself, they were on the same page. Wasn't it?

The next morning, Keely woke up feeling groggy from a lack of sleep and even more confused over Ethan's speedy retreat after one cup of hot cocoa. She'd sensed him pulling back before he'd taken the first sip. Out of self-preservation, when he'd started making noise about needing to get home, she urged him quickly along.

Shoving the disturbing man out of her mind, she focused on getting Felicity ready for school. The task was far more stressful and chaotic than feeding half the town on St. Patrick's Day. When she eventually steered into the school's carpool line, she discovered she'd forgotten to pack Felicity a lunch.

"I'll do better tomorrow," she promised as she handed over a five-dollar bill. "But you'll have to eat the school's food one more day."

"No worries. A lot of kids buy their lunch."

Not kids with mothers who owned a successful restaurant. Making a lunch was a way to show the little girl she meant to be more than a glorified babysitter. The Lord had brought Felicity into her life, and Keely would honor the privilege of mothering her by being, well, a good mother.

After she dropped Felicity off, the rest of Keely's morning went by quickly. She worked at her restaurant, falling back into a comfortable rhythm with her staff.

By the time most of the lunch crowd had cleared out, she was ready for a break. Actually, what she needed was chocolate.

"I'll be back in fifteen," she told her kitchen manager on her way out the door. She crossed

Main Street at a trot, then ducked inside Olivia's Sweet Shoppe.

The aroma of handcrafted chocolates beckoned her further inside. A cluster of café tables encouraged customers like her to sit, sip hot cocoa or enjoy the various chocolates and other treats available to the sugar enthusiast.

Busy helping a customer, Olivia looked modern and chic in her brown twill pants and a pink, fitted T-shirt with the store's logo scrolled across the front. Keely made eye contact with her friend, and then headed to the display case while she waited for Olivia to finish up with the sale.

The pleasant scent of chocolate flowed over her, making her aware she'd skipped lunch. As she snagged a sample of peppermint chocolate bark, her phone vibrated with an incoming text.

She glanced at the screen and shook her head at the message from Ethan, asking if he could skip the parade meeting tonight because Baloo will get lonely if I leave him on his own that long.

Choking on a laugh, she keyed in her response. Don't even think about bailing on me.

His return text had her rolling her eyes. Cut the poor dog a break. He's feeling needy lately.

She fired off another message. Are you still pouting over the camels?

I don't pout, was his reply.

Her fingers flew over the keyboard as she dared

him to prove it, by coming to the meeting and actually behaving himself for once.

Her phone rang a second later, the tune from the movie *Jaws* blaring out its ominous two-note warning. She punched the talk button. "I mean it, Ethan. You agreed to be on the committee and I'm not letting you back out now that the real work has begun."

A very low, very masculine sigh filled her ear.

"What's wrong? Got a hot date?" She regretted her words as soon as they came out of her mouth. Now he was going to think she was interested in him in *that way*.

"As a matter of fact…"

She could hear the snarky grin in his voice.

"I do."

"Oh." Disappointment rocked through her, which was really irritating. Ethan might be young, single, successful and good-looking, but now that she thought about it, Keely hadn't seen him with a woman outside of work-related events. She wondered what had changed.

"My date is with a large pepperoni pizza, my needy dog and the rest of the Broncos game I have recorded on my DVR."

The relief she felt came fast and hard, which irritated her even more. All she could manage was another breathless, "Oh."

His amused chuckle did annoying things to her heartbeat. "As much as I hate to admit this, Ethan,

I really need you to pull your weight on the committee. The parade route is long and winding, and you know Village Green better than most."

He paused for a long moment. "Fine," he said at last. "I'll be there."

"Don't make me come looking for you."

"I'm half tempted to skip the meeting, if only to see if you'd actually hunt me down."

"You wouldn't like it."

"Says you."

"Ethan—"

"Don't worry. I'll be at the meeting. I'll even bring pizza for the troops."

"You're a good man, Dr. Scott."

"About time you said so."

Both laughing, they disconnected the call at the same time.

What, she wondered, was that? If she didn't know better, she'd say Ethan had been flirting with her, and she with him.

She was still staring at the black screen when her friend came up beside her and pointed to the phone. "Bad news?"

"No." Keely lifted her head. "Why do you ask?"

"You're frowning."

She forced a smile that clearly failed to convince her friend. "Is it Felicity?" Olivia queried.

"No, she's good, and one of the reasons I stopped in." She juggled the phone in her hands. "I was thinking we could set up a sleepover for the girls this Saturday night."

"What a lovely idea." As they discussed the particulars, Olivia's worried expression stayed firmly in place.

"Keely? Are you sure there's nothing bothering you, something you'd like to share with your very best friend?"

"I'm fine. Just a little tired, if you must know."

"I don't doubt you're exhausted." She closed her hand on Keely's arm. "It's just…I don't quite know how to put this, so I'll say it plainly. I'm worried about you."

In that, at least, Keely could put her friend at ease. "My life has changed completely since Felicity moved in with me. And the transition hasn't been completely smooth."

"The change started before your cousin arrived." Olivia took both her hands. "Tell me what's made you so…distracted."

How did Keely explain something she hardly understood herself? Not without sharing the shift in her feelings for Ethan, feelings she was ruthlessly trying to restrain. "It's parade stuff, nothing I can't handle."

Sympathy replaced the worry in Olivia's eyes. "I take it my brother is still giving you a hard time about the camels."

"How on earth do you know about that?"

"Blame it on modern technology." Olivia laughed.

"The Village Green Facebook page has several posts about your argument. But don't take my word for it, see for yourself."

Keely thumbed open the appropriate app on her phone and scrolled through the posts. The comment about Ethan putting up a fight over camels pulling Santa's sleigh had three hundred and seventy-eight likes, fifty-nine comments and twelve shares. There was another post with an accompanying picture of Keely and Ethan standing toe-to-toe, caught in the middle of a stare down.

Oddly, instead of looking angry, they looked as if they were having fun, as if they were flirting instead of arguing. The post coined their conflict as *Camelgate* and asked the question *Will we see camels walking the streets of Village Green this Christmas Eve? Or will the good doctor get his way?*

There were four hundred and thirty-two comments already debating the issue, most siding with Keely.

Shaking her head, she closed the app. "People in this town have way too much time on their hands."

"All right, out with it." Olivia pointed an accusing finger at her. "How did you scam Ethan into working on the parade?"

Keely didn't like the implication that she'd twisted Ethan's arm to get him to cooperate. Sure, she'd all but dared him, but he was his own man. He could have said no at any point. "You've got it all wrong. It was your brother's idea to give back to the community."

"Nope, not buying it, what do you have on him?"

"Nothing."

"Oh, it's something, all right."

Irritated on Ethan's behalf, she frowned at her friend. "You're not being fair to your brother. He's devoted to pulling his weight on the committee."

"Look at you, taking up for him. I simply don't know what to think."

"What does that mean?"

Olivia cocked her head. "As long as I've known you, you've never once come to my brother's defense before."

Was she really that contrary when it came to Ethan that his own sister found her defense of his character suspicious? The question haunted her long after she left the chocolate shop.

En route back to the restaurant, Olivia's words floated around in Keely's head. *You've never once come to my brother's defense before.*

Sadly, her friend was right. For years, she'd chosen to see Ethan through the eyes of a humiliated teenager. The hostility hadn't been completely one-sided. But, to his credit, Ethan had made the first step toward reconciliation. It was now up to Keely to adjust her attitude toward the man.

It helped that he'd shown her a new side of himself recently. He'd trudged through a blanket of snow, twice, to check on a sick child, then lent that same scared little girl his dog just to keep her from feeling lonely.

Keely recognized the flutter in her heart. She'd felt it before. She'd been thirteen, infatuated with a boy five years older than her. Falling for Ethan—again—could very well end just as badly as before. With her humiliated and Ethan completely clueless.

No, thank you. Not only wouldn't she do that to herself, but she wouldn't drag Felicity through the emotional maelstrom, either. Perhaps, one day, Keely would fall in love again, with a man who loved her as much as she loved him.

That man would not be Ethan Scott.

Chapter Ten

Not long after disconnecting with Keely, Ethan's phone buzzed again. His gut rolled at the familiar name and number blinking across the screen. He hadn't spoken to Tracy's mother in months, and only three times since the funeral.

Between their last conversation and now, he'd spent more time thinking about his lovely neighbor than the woman he'd vowed to cherish all his life. He felt like a coldhearted jerk.

Nevertheless, he let the call go to voice mail and shoved his past in the dark recesses of his mind. He spent the rest of the afternoon seeing patients. Though he had no idea why, several of them thanked him for his service before he redirected the conversation back to them.

Curiosity had him stopping Connor in the hallway. "What's with all the outpouring of public gratitude for my service?"

Connor's eyebrows shot up. "You're really getting outpourings of gratitude?"

Ethan nodded.

"Then let me add my thanks to the mix, because, dude, when you step up, *you step up*. Man to man, what made you do it?"

Ethan had no idea what Connor was talking about. "Define...*it*."

"Word around town is that you're officially working on the Christmas parade."

"It's true, I am...now, wait just a minute. How do you know this? I've only attended two meetings." As soon as he said the words, he remembered this was Village Green. Gossip traveled faster than the speed of light.

"Village Green's Facebook page is a plethora of information." Connor said this with absolutely no sarcasm in his voice.

It was all in his eyes.

"Village Green has a Facebook page? Why?"

"I would think it's self-explanatory," Connor said, chuckling. "You should check it out sometime. There are even pictures from a parade meeting. One in particular has the town talking, for good reason."

Ethan stared at his partner, partly baffled, partly horrified the Village Green's grapevine had gone digital. And there were pictures. He shuddered. "I'll pass, thanks."

"If it was anyone else, I'd say our newly elected

mayor engaged in a fair amount of arm-twisting." Connor shook his head, obviously baffled. "So, tell me, what happened?"

"Wrong place, wrong time."

"I'm thinking there's more to the story, and your lovely neighbor is at the heart of it."

When it came to him and Keely, there was always more to the story. Ethan had been denying the truth of that for months, avoiding her in an attempt to keep her out of his head, and possibly even his heart.

"Well, however it came about, I'm glad you're getting reconnected in the community. It's been a long time coming." Connor clasped his shoulder. "Welcome back to the living."

Ethan flinched. "What's that supposed to mean?"

"You know exactly what it means. Take it from someone who knows, you've been among the walking dead long enough."

Ethan bristled. "It's called mourning. I lost the love of my life." He clenched his teeth. "It's only right to honor her memory."

"By not living your life? By holing yourself up in your house every night, going out only when it's required? That's not honoring her memory, it's living in fear."

"What do you know about it?"

As the words slid past his lips, Ethan knew they were a mistake. Of course Conner understood

Ethan's private pain. His friend had lost his wife to cancer, and had spent three years living solely for his daughters and not for himself. Only after Olivia came into his life did things change.

"You want to honor Tracy's memory," Connor said, his tone sympathetic, "start living again, Ethan. It's the best advice I can give."

He knew his friend was probably right. And yet he couldn't help thinking this conversation was somehow a betrayal to everything Tracy had been to him. "I didn't ask for your advice."

"No, you didn't." Connor blew out a sharp breath of air, started to say more, but Tasha chose that moment to poke her head out from exam room 5.

She pointed at Ethan, then Connor. "Move it, boys. We have patients waiting and a tight schedule to keep."

Duly chastised, Ethan and Connor went their separate ways. Despite the busy afternoon, Ethan left the office with plenty of time to feed and walk Baloo before the parade meeting.

On his way to City Hall, he stopped in Pizza Italiano to pick up the promised pizzas. As he waited for his order, Connor's words came back to him. *You want to honor Tracy's memory, start living again.*

Wasn't that what he was doing? By serving on the parade committee?

Somehow he didn't think that was what Connor meant.

Ethan arrived on time. Flicka saw him the moment he entered the conference room.

"Dr. Ethan. Dr. Ethan." She skidded to a stop inches from him, then eyed the stack of boxes in his hands with obvious interest. "What kind of pizza did you bring?"

He set the boxes on the table. "There's one cheese pizza, one with everything on it and two with pepperoni."

"I looooove pepperoni." Clearly delighted, Flicka thanked him with a fast hug full of little-girl ferocity.

Emotion simmered just beneath his oh-so-calm surface, battling its way to freedom. *Start living again.*

His heart ached with a twinge of yearning, as though what he really wanted was within his grasp, if only he had the courage to reach for it.

He carefully set the girl away from him and focused on opening the lid of the first pizza box. The rest of the committee swarmed around the food.

Happy for the distraction, Ethan swapped greetings, surprised at how comfortable he felt around these women, solidarity through their joint efforts to put on the best parade the town had ever seen.

He took a quick head count and noticed a glaring omission. He sent a hopeful look in Keely's direction. "Lacy not coming tonight?"

"Oh, she's coming, but she's running late, as

usual. If she's not here in ten minutes, we'll start without her."

Nancy Watson, a middle-aged woman once friends with Ethan's mother, went in search of plates and napkins. Mrs. Sweeny, his high school geometry teacher, took orders for anyone who wanted a drink from the soda machine.

As Ethan interacted with the rest of the women in the room, he thought he heard a click that sounded like the camera app on a smartphone. He remembered Connor's words about the Village Green Facebook page. *There are even pictures.*

Feeling mildly violated, Ethan claimed his usual seat beside Flicka. He quickly concluded she was feeling okay. Her color was good and her eyes clear. He felt it safe to ask, "How was school today?"

"Great." She beamed at him. "Did I tell you that Keely and I are going to pick out our Christmas tree this weekend? We're not getting a plastic one, either, but a real live one."

"Make sure it's a Colorado blue spruce, or nothing at all."

"Okay." She dropped her gaze to her lap, but not before Ethan caught the agony in her eyes.

He'd seen the same expression in the mirror in those early weeks after Tracy's death. Sorrow, pain, lost hope. Poor kid.

He wanted to pull the little girl close and tell her everything was going to be all right. But he didn't know that for certain, and he didn't make promises he couldn't keep.

"What's wrong, Flicka?"

She glanced up, her watery eyes glistening under the lights overhead.

"I want to get my mom and Keely Christmas presents." She whispered the words so softly he had to lean forward to hear. "But I don't know how I can."

Relief washed through him. The problem had an easy solution. "I'll take you shopping."

The storm clouds disappeared from her expression. "You…you don't mind?"

"Not at all." Actually, he hated shopping, and couldn't think of a worse activity than flitting from store to store in search of a perfect gift. But the kid had a dilemma and Ethan was in a position to solve it.

"We'll go Saturday. It's my turn to see patients in the morning, but after that I'm free the rest of the day."

"Oh, Dr. Ethan, thank you. Thank you so much."

"You're welcome." He shifted in his chair, wondering how he'd managed to get himself in this deep, this fast.

Panic tried to take root. He'd done nothing out of the ordinary, he told himself. His offer to take the kid shopping wasn't personal. It was what he did. He solved problems.

Keep telling yourself that, Doctor.

Fortunately, Keely called the meeting to order. "The route coordinator and I will do a walk through town next week." She caught Ethan's eye. "If that works for you."

He nodded.

"Great."

The individual reports were next. Because he was the newest member of the team, Ethan went last. "I've met with the Village Green police and fire departments. We're good to go on security and ready for any unforeseen emergencies. The route is also confirmed."

He had Flicka pass out copies of the route map, then wrapped up his report and smiled at Keely. "Back to you."

"Where are we on the camel situation?"

A hush fell over the room and all heads turned to him. "Same as we were last time you asked, and the time before that."

"You haven't even tried to find them, have you?"

"Actually, I have." He lifted the lid of his laptop and opened his email. "As of this morning, I've found a company willing to lend us camels for the day. I'm waiting to hear on the cost for transportation before I commit."

Fully aware all gazes were fixed on him and Keely, he shut the lid of his laptop and smiled smugly at her.

She held his stare. "When will you know for certain?"

He gave a quick, succinct answer. "Soon."

"Give me a ballpark."

The woman was relentless. "Two to three days."

"We're running out of time, Ethan."

Her distress was evident and Ethan realized getting the camels was important to her. "I'll make it happen, Keely." This time, his smile was sincere. "I promise."

A few female sighs filled the room.

"Thank you, Ethan. I trust you won't let me down."

When she looked at him that way, with confidence and respect, he knew he'd pick up the camels himself if that was what it took to have her think that highly of him.

The door swung open and Lacy rushed into the room, drawing all eyes in her direction. The woman certainly knew how to make an entrance. She tossed down her purse. "We have a problem."

"What sort of problem?" Keely asked in a strained voice.

"We no longer have a Santa."

"Oh no!"

Ethan couldn't blame Keely for that small moment of alarm. Santa was the highlight of the parade. First the camels, and now Santa?

"What happened, Lacy? Ralph Donovan has always done such a great job in years past. He—" Keely broke off, then glanced at Felicity. "Sweetie, would you mind getting me a soda from the machine?"

"Okay."

Once the child left the room, a dollar bill clutched in her palm, Keely addressed Lacy once again. "You told us at the last meeting that Ralph was confirmed."

Lacy lifted a silk-clad shoulder. "He wants nothing to do with a sleigh being pulled by camels. He says they spit."

Ethan gave Keely an ironic tilt of his head. It took everything in him not to say I told you so.

Hips swaying, Lacy maneuvered around the table and then sat in Felicity's empty seat. "You know, Ethan, I'm thinking you could rock a Santa suit."

Caught completely off guard by such a ridiculous suggestion, he gaped at the woman a full two seconds. Mistake.

Warming to the idea, the committee began talking over one another, delightfully hashing out the possibility of Ethan taking over for Ralph. They tossed out a large number of pros, a few cons, then a whole lot more pros.

Keely attempted to regain order. She even tried to explain why Ethan couldn't possibly be the route coordinator *and* Santa, without success.

Short of coming off as a Scrooge, Ethan was stuck. The news was probably already up on Facebook. He didn't know whether to say ho-ho-ho or bah humbug.

"You okay with this?" Keely asked him over the excited chatter.

He shrugged.

"Okay, then, problem solved. We have us a Santa after all."

Cheers erupted in the room.

Two days after the disastrous parade meeting, Ethan still wasn't sure how he'd ended up with the conspicuous job of Santa, in a sleigh pulled by camels. Camels he was now tasked with finding because he'd promised Keely he wouldn't let her down.

The woman standing beside him outside Village Green's animal shelter had to realize this was her fault. She'd clearly lost control of her committee. By the glances she threw his way, no doubt Keely was waiting for him to back out at any minute.

Ethan could ease her mind, let her know he would follow through on his word, but what would be the fun in that?

Just to annoy her, he released a long-suffering sigh.

"I'm really sorry, Ethan. If you don't want to be Santa I'm sure I'll find someone else."

There was a note of desperation in her voice. Obviously, locating another Santa at this late date wouldn't be easy.

"It's no big deal, Keely, a couple hours on a parade float." He'd made a promise. He would follow through, unless he could con Ryder into filling in for him. One Scott brother was the same as the other.

Keely blinked up at him, her eyes soft, a little dreamy. Had he put that look on her face?

"Come on. Let's get out of this frigid wind and pick out Flicka's Christmas present."

They entered the animal shelter in silence. The foyer was decorated with pinecones, garland, red poinsettia plants and a large wreath on the front of the welcome desk.

The place might look like Christmas. It did not smell like Christmas. The scent of industrial cleaner failed to mask the fragrant odor of Eau de Wet Dog.

"Oh, Ethan, I have no idea how I'm going to choose."

"That's why I'm here."

Nodding, she started for the desk.

Ethan stopped her with a hand on her arm. "Before we go any further, I want you to repeat after me. 'I can only get one.'"

She made a face. "Is that really necessary?"

The innocent question told him she'd never been inside an animal shelter. He had an instant need to protect her, to bundle her up and hustle her out of the building. With her big soft heart, this process was going to be hard on her. For days, maybe even weeks, her dreams were going to be haunted by all the little furry faces she had to leave behind.

"Say the words, Keely." He pressed his face inches from hers. "'I can only get one'."

"Oh, honestly." She rolled her eyes. "'I can only get one.'"

"Again, and this time with conviction."

"I. Can. Only. Get. One."

"Now you're ready." He stepped back. "After you."

Head tilted at a haughty angle, she approached the welcome desk and stated her desire to adopt a dog. The teenage girl behind the counter handed them over to an older woman with a wiry build, thick glasses and gray, springy hair. She introduced herself as Margo.

"I'm Keely and this is Ethan."

"Follow me." As Margo escorted them into the kennel area, she fired off several initial questions, then asked, "Is there a specific type of dog you're looking for?"

"Not really. I originally thought I wanted a puppy, but I'm open to other options."

"That's good to know. Sometimes the older dogs get ignored this time of year." Margo unlocked a gate and led the way into a long walkway with wire kennels on either side.

Keely entered next, Ethan right behind her.

Even from this distance, they were confronted with a menagerie of breeds, sizes and ages. Ethan couldn't stand the neediness, the sorrow, the silent plea for rescue. He hardened his heart to their plight. Either that or Baloo would have a sibling before nightfall.

Evidently facing her own struggles, Keely muttered, "I can only get one. I can only get one. I can only get one."

He took her hand. "We can come back another time."

"No." She drew in a sharp breath. "I want to do this, for Felicity."

"For Felicity," he repeated, even as he felt the tug of a dozen conflicting emotions in his gut.

Like so many of the animals behind the cage doors, Ethan felt abandoned, with an empty future ahead of him. He could never reclaim the dreams he'd lost. But maybe, like some of the animals here, he could reach for a new one.

Was he ready to take the risk? To confront the possibility of another loss, for the sake of what he could gain? He thought maybe he was. But if he took the leap, what would it mean to Tracy's memory?

If he were a praying man, now would be a good time to lift up a petition for clarity.

Keely pulled her hand free, took a deep breath and then began the arduous process of choosing a dog. She moved from cage to cage, stopping, assessing, then repeating the process on the other side of the aisle.

Ethan felt her internal battle as if it were his own.

They came to the end of the kennel area. Keely

retraced her steps. On this second pass, she paused at only one cage. For several seconds she studied the brown-and-white dog with the long, shiny coat and soulful black eyes. He—or she—wasn't quite a puppy, but not fully mature, either, probably somewhere between five and six months old. The handwritten placard on the kennel read Cupcake, Male, Mixed Breed.

Keely lowered herself to her knees and started speaking softly to the docile animal. The poor little guy had a distant look in his eyes and a collapsed posture, clear signs of mistreatment from his previous owner.

"I don't know, Keely, he seems pretty timid. If he's been abused he could prove difficult to train."

Waving off his concerns, she swung her gaze to Margo. "What's his history?"

When the woman gave Keely a glowing report, Ethan asked the most pertinent question. "How long has he been here?"

"Nearly three months," she admitted.

Not a good sign. Ethan expressed his concerns.

Margo glowered. "I blame it on the internet. There are too many how-to-pick-a-dog articles out there warning people off timid animals like Cupcake. All he needs is a little love, a safe environment and some patience."

Ethan wasn't convinced.

Reading his hesitation accurately, Keely parked

her hands on her hips. "Remind me again about the day you found Baloo in Afghanistan."

On one of his many lunch breaks at Senor O'Toole's, Ethan had told Keely how he'd found Baloo in a burned-out hut, cowering in a corner. The dog had been even more timid than Cupcake.

"I seem to remember you saying something about Baloo blossoming once he knew he was safe and loved."

Point taken. Three years later, Baloo was one of the friendliest dogs in Village Green. He never met a person—or animal—he couldn't get along with, including cats.

Keely leaned into his personal space. "You think Baloo knows he was rescued?"

The woman was—no pun intended—like a dog with a bone.

"You win." Ethan lifted his hands in surrender. "It's your choice."

She pointed to Cupcake. "I'd like to take him into one of the get-to-know-you rooms."

An hour later, paperwork complete, Ethan drove away from the animal shelter with Flicka's new dog tucked in a borrowed carrier on the backseat of his SUV.

They made a stop at a local pet store, then were back on the road. Halfway into their neighborhood, Keely placed a hand on his right biceps. "Thank you again for agreeing to keep Cupcake at your house until Christmas morning. Felicity will be so surprised when you bring him over."

Ethan had tried to talk himself out of making the offer. Yet he'd made it anyway. "Baloo can use the company."

"It's not too late to change your mind. I can ask Beau to keep Cupcake at his house." She pulled out her cell phone, waved it back and forth. "Just say the word."

"Don't call your brother. It's less than two weeks to Christmas. What could possibly go wrong?" A thousand things, he knew, but a lot could go right.

Tucking her phone back in her purse, Keely relaxed. "At least let me come over and take care of him."

That was precisely what Ethan didn't want. Having Keely in his house daily was too cozy, too couple-like.

"You'll hardly know I'm there," she persisted.

He opened his mouth to volunteer Ryder for the job, but found himself saying, "I'll get you a key to the back door."

Chapter Eleven

After a few sniffs and a handful of circling each other, Cupcake and Baloo became fast friends. It seemed the puppy's transition was going to be easier than Felicity's. That was something to celebrate. Wanting to share her pleasure with Ethan, Keely glanced over at him.

He wasn't watching the dogs. He was watching her, closely. And yet his expression was carefully neutral.

"Thanks again for letting Cupcake bunk at your house."

"No problem." He flashed a smile, the one that turned her stomach into a trampoline for an entire family of butterflies. "I kind of like the little guy."

Reaching down, he scratched the puppy's head.

"Don't get too attached, Dr. Scott. Cupcake is an O'Toole man through and through."

Ethan's smile moved into his eyes. "Please tell me you're going to change his name."

"I'll let Felicity decide."

"I suppose that makes sense." Eyes locked with hers, he straightened. He took a step toward her, just one, yet the air in the room suddenly changed, becoming charged with energy.

Their relationship was shifting into new territory, though she doubted neither of them would admit that out loud.

He took another step. She took one herself, until they were standing face-to-face, mere inches apart, so close that she could see the countless shades of blue in his eyes.

"Is this a bad idea?" she asked him.

"Probably."

Not sure if they were talking about the puppy, or something else entirely, she held her position.

Ethan remained unmoving, as well. The tension was thick in the air between them, but not altogether unpleasant.

"We should head back to work."

Breathless for no good reason, Keely nodded. The silent standoff continued. Neither of them moved.

Then Ethan's head drew a shade closer. He was going to kiss her. She didn't know whether to be overjoyed or terrified. Holding her breath, she remained steady, waiting, watching.

His lips touched hers, barely a whisper; then he snapped back and put a polite distance between them. "I'll...uh, get that key I promised."

She choked on a breathless sigh. "I'll wait here."

The air felt lighter with him out of the room. Staring at nothing in particular, she reached up and touched her mouth. Ethan had barely pressed his lips to hers and yet the moment had felt special, life altering.

Needing something to do with her hands, she reached down to pet the puppy. Ethan returned with the key and handed it to her.

Their fingers were still touching when Ryder shuffled into the kitchen. Keely jumped back, away from Ethan. She didn't know why she felt so guilty. Ryder hadn't even noticed her yet.

Sleep-rumpled, his hair sticking out from nearly every angle, Ryder let out a jaw-cracking yawn. He wore faded jeans that looked a million years old, an equally ancient sweatshirt and a tired grimace.

The Scott men looked alike, but this one favored Ethan the most. They had the same cobalt-blue eyes, long black eyelashes and bold slash of eyebrows beneath a full head of black hair.

Ryder swept a glance over the room in general. "Morning."

Voice strained, Keely responded in kind.

"Keely?" His gaze narrowed, and he glanced from Keely to Ethan and then back to her. "What are you doing in my kitchen?"

"She's with me." Ethan maneuvered to stand slightly in front of her, as if to shield her from his own brother.

"Let me get this straight." Ryder stared at his brother. "You're in the same room with Keely... willingly?"

Well, ouch. Didn't take a rocket scientist to decipher the meaning behind Ryder's shocked reaction.

Keely didn't know why she was so surprised. Prior to her call for help with Felicity, Ethan had made a point of keeping his distance from her. She'd avoided him, as well.

Still, Ryder's words hurt.

She told herself the opinion of others didn't matter. She didn't need to win earthly favor. Only what God thought of her truly mattered. Except there were times when Keely did care what others thought of her. What did that say about her?

Not liking this insight into her character, she cut a quick glance at Ethan. His eyes were on his brother and he'd flattened his lips into a hard, grim line. He looked as though he was about to tear into Ryder. On her behalf.

How utterly fascinating. And really, really sweet.

She choked out what she hoped was a mild laugh and adopted a casual stance. "Come on, Ryder. Ethan comes into my restaurant at least three times a week."

"Sometimes more than that. I enjoy Keely's company."

Ryder scoffed at this. "Since when?"

Keely flicked another glance at Ethan. Quiet, calm, expression closed, he held her gaze.

She shifted her attention back to Ryder. He was leaning against the counter, eyes on her. But where Ethan's gaze was inscrutable, Ryder's was full of brotherly concern. For her.

"Don't read too much into this, Ryder. Ethan and I were just dropping off my little cousin's Christmas present."

On cue, a happy yip cut through the tension in the room.

Ryder zeroed in on the canine wrestling match at his feet. "Either I'm seeing double or there are two dogs at my feet."

"Ryder, meet Cupcake." She reached down and picked up the puppy, holding him as much as a shield as a means to give the man a better look. "Felicity's Christmas present."

Ryder's face went blank. "Who's Felicity?"

"Keely's cousin. I told you about her." Ethan's words were meant as an explanation, but sounded more like a scold. "She's the little girl that moved in with Keely last weekend."

"I thought her name was Flicka."

"Felicity *is* Flicka. They're one and the same."

"Right, got it." Yawning, Ryder ran a hand over his tired face. "What time is it, anyway?"

Ethan glanced at the chunky black watch on his wrist. "Quarter till eleven."

"Earlier than I thought. No wonder I feel like someone parked a tractor on my head."

By the gravelly quality of his voice and the half-glazed eyes, it was clear they'd interrupted Ryder's sleep. Keely winced in chagrin. "Tell me we didn't wake you."

"Nope, hunger woke me." He reached for an apple, took a loud, crunching bite. He continued staring at Keely, then Ethan, then Keely again. "You two, together in the same room. Huh."

Ethan made a sound in his throat that was just short of a growl. "Go back to bed, Ryder."

Apple in hand, Ryder headed toward the living room, then paused in the doorway. His gaze dipped to the dog in her arms, then returned to her face. He appeared about to say something, then seemed to change his mind. "Bye, Keely."

"Bye, Ryder."

She waited until he was out of earshot before breaking her silence. "That was awkward."

"A little bit."

Sighing, she hugged the puppy closer. He gave her chin a swipe of his pink tongue, then settled comfortably in her arms.

"Ryder's been working the night shift all week. His internal clock is way off. He probably won't even remember seeing you this morning."

She let out a mirthless laugh. "A gal can hope."

He took the puppy from her arms and gently set him on the floor. "Let's finish getting Flicka's dog settled in and then I'll drive you back to the restaurant."

As if by silent agreement, they said nothing more about the kiss that, from Keely's point of view, wasn't really a kiss. Like a well-oiled machine they worked in tandem making Cupcake comfortable in his temporary home.

Back in her restaurant, Keely walked into the kitchen and did what she did best. She took charge. Elbow deep in orders, she told herself nothing had changed between her and Ethan.

Deep down, she knew that wasn't true.

Everything had changed.

At the memory of being wrapped in his arms for those brief seconds, feeling warm and safe and cherished, her eyes shut of their own accord. Ethan's lips had barely touched hers, but she'd felt treasured on a level she hadn't realized existed.

Had Ethan experienced a similar connection?

The question unsettled her. Because whether or not her handsome neighbor had been affected by her, she'd been affected by him. There could be no going back to the way things were between them. Of course, that didn't mean Keely couldn't try.

With renewed resolve, she opened her eyes and went to work feeding the hungry lunch crowd.

Saturday morning dawned cloudless and bitter cold. Although Ethan would rather stay in bed, he had two dogs requiring his attention. He dressed quickly, then trudged down the stairs and into the kitchen. Pink-tinted light bathed the room in a soft, welcoming glow.

Not yet fully awake, he glanced at the thermometer as he filled the dogs' empty food bowls. Overnight, the outside temperature had dipped to an inhuman five degrees Fahrenheit.

Once they'd consumed their breakfast, both animals gave him identical expressions of need. "Hang tight, boys."

He pulled out his phone and texted Keely, asking if the coast was clear. She sent him a quick thumbs-up emoticon, followed by three smiley faces.

"We're good to go."

Shoving his arms in his heaviest coat, he opened the back door and stepped back. Baloo and Cupcake bulleted past him. Both dogs seemed oblivious of the dangerously cold air. Blowing into his cupped palms, Ethan pulled up the hood and huddled deeper inside his coat.

The sun had barely made its appearance in the east, but the sky was already a spectacular explosion of color. Ethan might not be on the best of terms with the Lord, but that didn't mean he couldn't appreciate the artistry of His handiwork. Looking at the wonder of God's creation, he didn't doubt He existed.

What he had a harder time grasping was why the Lord allowed some people to die young, and others to live into old age. Why cancer ravaged an otherwise healthy body, yet a person with terrible eating habits never got sick.

It all seemed so random. Ethan couldn't begin to comprehend God's unfathomable ways, or understand why the Lord allowed tragic car accidents to happen to good people. *Why, Lord?*

He'd asked the question a thousand times, had received the same silent response. Familiar agitation reared. He tried to pace off the sensation in the thick snow. The troubling doubt only grew, stretching and snapping inside his gut.

The creak of door hinges had him looking across Keely's backyard. Bundled in a thick, oversize coat and snow boots, she exited her house and trotted over to him. Welcoming the interruption, he focused solely on the woman approaching him with a smile.

Keely's face was free of cosmetics, and her hair was a red, flaming cloud of curls framing her exquisite face.

She'd never looked more beautiful. The last time they'd been this close, this alone, Ethan had pulled her into his arms and briefly kissed her. He'd tried to put the moment out of his mind, had nearly succeeded, but now that she stood barely a foot away he could think of nothing else.

"Hey," he said around the lump lodged in his throat.

"Hey."

They stared at each other for several beats. Her eyes were warm, full of unspoken words. His heart squeezed.

She shifted her stance. "You ready for tonight?"

He lifted an eyebrow.

"The walk-through of the parade route."

"Right, yeah, sure. Flicka coming, too?"

"She's spending the night with Molly and Megan. It'll just be the two of us."

He didn't know whether to be pleased or worried. The kid acted as a nice buffer. Cupcake, misjudging speed and distance, slammed into Keely's booted ankles.

"Well, hello there." She scooped up the puppy.

Clearly happy to see her, the animal showered her with doggy kisses. Her throaty laugh added to Ethan's agitation.

He looked away, fought for control, searched his mind for an innocuous topic. "Where's Flicka?"

"Fast asleep." She dodged another round of sloppy dog kisses, then set the puppy on the ground. "It was nice of you to offer to take her Christmas shopping, but it's not necessary. I'm free this afternoon. I can—"

"She asked me for a reason, Keely." He watched, mildly affronted, as her smile dropped into a scowl. "You got a problem with me spending time alone with Flicka?"

"I trust you with her, it's just…" Sighing, she twisted the tails of her scarf between her fingers.

"I don't understand why she asked you to take her shopping instead of me."

"Think about it, Keely. Why wouldn't she want you to take her Christmas shopping?"

"I don't know, I—Oh." She lifted her hands, let them flutter to her sides. "*Oh*. She wants to buy me a gift."

He tapped her on the nose. "Bingo."

"And you agreed to help her pick out my present?"

"Two for two."

"Oh, Ethan." She gave him a watery smile. "How completely, utterly sweet of you both."

Giving him no chance to respond, she leaped forward, planted a brief kiss on his lips, then bounced out of reach.

His heart took a direct hit.

He'd always had a soft spot for Keely. Even as kids, he'd considered it his duty to look out for her, to protect her. But this warmth spreading through him felt like something more than duty, something more than friendship, something…lasting.

Every muscle in his back tightened.

"I should get back inside, before Felicity wakes up and comes looking for me."

Cheeks bright pink, she gave him a smile that nearly brought him to his knees. At her back door, she paused and then pulled out her phone. Her thumbs tapped across the screen.

At the same moment she lifted her head, his

phone buzzed with an incoming text. He didn't have to guess who it was from.

Smiling like a sap, he retrieved his phone and read Keely's message. Thanks for being so wonderful with Felicity. xoxox

The fact that she put her gratitude in writing, where he could see it for as long as he kept the text on his phone, touched him in ways he couldn't explain. But it was the *x*'s and *o*'s—hugs and kisses—that really got to him. His heart pounded so hard he felt each beat at the base of his neck.

He looked up, expecting to catch her watching for his reaction, but she'd already vanished inside her house.

He lowered his head again, noticed the voice mail from Mrs. Jenkins still waiting for him. After herding the dogs back inside the house, then making sure they had fresh water, he forced himself to listen to the message.

Bracing himself as if heading into battle, he punched the screen, then pulled the phone up to his ear.

Unmistakable sadness flowed through him as the familiar voice said, "Ethan, hi, it's me, Phyllis, Tracy's mother."

She spoke with a tentative rasp, as if there were a possibility he would forget who she was and how they were connected.

He listened to the rest of the voice mail like a man facing a firing squad. It wasn't until he put the phone back in his pocket that he realized the magnitude of the woman's request and what it would cost him. Tracy's mother wanted him at yet another memorial service for her daughter. She also wished for Ethan to be the one to scatter Tracy's ashes over her favorite lake.

He'd already said goodbye to his fiancée at her military funeral. He couldn't go through a second ceremony. He shouldn't have to, *none* of them should, which was why he'd urged her family to scatter her ashes that day. Her mother had protested, claiming she wanted her daughter with her a little while longer.

Now, nearly eighteen months later, Phyllis was finally ready to let Tracy go. Ethan was happy she was seeking closure, but he wanted no part of the process. He deleted the message.

The rest of the morning, he focused on work. He gave his patients his full attention. Whenever he found himself with a free moment, his thoughts wanted to dwell on the past. Yet every time he thought of Tracy, he struggled to bring up a clear image.

To make matters worse, Keely's likeness kept encroaching at the oddest moments. More and more he saw past the bristle and droll humor to the sweet, vulnerable woman beneath.

He shoved both women out of his head.

At five minutes to noon, he saw his last patient for the day. Mrs. Collier was an eighty-eight-year-old woman with a bad heart, struggling to survive on Social Security, and had a penchant for making him cookies as payment for his services. The old girl couldn't hear half of what he said. But he liked her.

When she left his office Ethan was in possession of a dozen cookies and a lighter heart. He walked the block and half to Senor O'Toole's. The place was swarming with customers, which suited his purposes perfectly. He stole Flicka away after a quick, perfunctory conversation with Keely.

One block later, he escorted the little girl into the first, and hopefully last, shop of the day. The Emporium was touted as Village Green's premier gift shop, specializing in everything from vintage tea sets to antique hair clips to all things female.

According to Ethan's sister, this was *the* place to buy a special gift for a woman. Flicka seemed to agree. Her delighted chatter filled the store.

"There are so many choices," she breathed.

That was an understatement.

It took less than two minutes for Ethan to realize he was in over his head. He was just about to call in the big guns, aka his sister, Olivia, when a teenage girl with a mouthful of braces approached him and Flicka. "How can I help you?"

Ethan let out a breath of relief. "We're looking for a Christmas gift for a woman."

"Actually, we're looking for two gifts," Flicka corrected. "One for my mom and one for my cousin Keely 'cause I love her and she's getting me a real tree. Isn't that cool?"

"Very." The salesgirl asked a few questions about both women, then began guiding Flicka through the store.

Happy to hand over the reins, Ethan wandered around on his own. A display of porcelain dolls caught his eye. Impressed with the intricacy of their clothes, he moved closer. One in particular pulled at him. The curly blond hair and big blue eyes looked so much like Flicka it was as if the kid had personally modeled for the doll-maker.

"Hey, Flicka, look at this." He plucked the toy off the table and presented it to the girl.

"She's super pretty." With tentative fingers, she reached out and touched the lacy green dress. "Hey, she kind of looks like me. Can we get her for my mom?"

He had no idea if a woman in prison was allowed such a luxury, but this was Flicka's decision. They'd figure out the logistics later. "If that's what you want."

She considered the doll with a thoughtful expression.

"Did you know my mommy is in prison?" Dropping her hand, she rolled her big, innocent eyes up to him. "She stole money that wasn't hers."

At the matter-of-fact delivery of this piece of information, Ethan's gut twisted so hard he had to swallow to catch his breath. "I'm sorry, Flicka."

"Me, too." She heaved another sigh. "Keely says everyone makes mistakes and my mommy is real sorry for what she did."

"I'm sure she is."

"If we get this doll for her, then maybe, when she's lonely and misses me, she can hug her real hard and not be so sad."

Throat thick, Ethan smoothed a hand over the bent head. The kid might as well have reached inside his chest and ripped out his heart. "That's a nice thought."

"So I can get this doll for my mom?"

"Consider it done."

The very corner of her mouth turned up. "Now I just have to find something for Keely."

As she headed over to a table with women's scarves and jewelry, Ethan fully understood Keely's desire to make this Christmas special for Flicka. She was such a great kid, with a tender, thoughtful heart. She deserved the best in life and definitely a great holiday season.

Maybe he could help with a little recon. He drew near the kid. "Have you thought about what you want for Christmas?"

"Oh, yes. I think about it all the time." Her eyes settled on him with a clarity that gave him a bad feeling in the pit of his stomach. "I want a daddy of my very own."

"Is that so?" he croaked out.

"I've never had a daddy before." The wistful

look she sent him shot past every defense he'd erected around his heart.

Ethan desperately wanted to make this child happy, but he couldn't give her what she wanted. It would be wrong to lead her on for even a minute. He tried to diffuse the situation.

"With Christmas only a few weeks away," he said slowly, choosing his words carefully, "it's kind of short notice. I don't think we'll be able to find you a daddy by then."

"I guess that makes sense." Shoulders slumped, head lowered, she rummaged through the scarves with lifeless flicks.

The kid's sorrow twisted Ethan's gut in all kinds of knots. Something stirred inside him, something stronger than frustration. Panic, or a desperate desire to fulfill her wish personally?

That kind of thinking would only end in disappointment for them all, especially Flicka. Again, Ethan redirected the conversation. "What else is on your Christmas list?"

Her hand paused. "Well…if I can't have a daddy, then there's only one other gift I want."

"What would that be?"

"A puppy."

Chapter Twelve

"Have fun, sweetie." Keely waved to a grinning Felicity as the child climbed into Olivia's SUV behind the Mitchell twins. Felicity's blond curls were loose and blowing across her face, her expression full of excitement for her sleepover.

So different from the little girl Keely had picked up at the Denver Airport the day after Thanksgiving. Felicity had come off the plane wearing dark shadows beneath her sad, red-rimmed eyes. She'd been wary of Keely at first, full of pain, but determined to make the most of her situation with the resilience that only came from the innocence of youth.

Barely three weeks in Village Green and Felicity was starting to look and act like a normal child, no dark circles under her eyes, much less hidden pain in their depths, and for that Keely lifted up a prayer of thanksgiving.

As Olivia's black SUV turned the corner and

the taillights disappeared from sight, Keely went back inside her restaurant.

Checking her watch, she gasped. She barely had time to get home, tame her unruly hair and apply fresh makeup before Ethan picked her up to walk the parade route. As she hurried home, she admitted, if only to herself, that she was looking forward to spending the evening with him.

A little hum of excitement sounded in her throat. Her relationship with her neighbor was long and complicated, made up of tension and laughter and a slew of emotions difficult to describe. There was a lot of water beneath their bridge, spiked with hurt feelings on her side, masculine wariness on his.

Keely didn't blame Ethan for her perceived hurts from the past. Well, okay, she didn't blame him anymore. Sighing, she stared at her image in the mirror of her bathroom, seeing the child she'd been, not the woman she'd become.

She'd grown up shy and awkward in her own skin. Her twin brother had been the opposite. Beau had been born cool, with an easiness that people gravitated toward.

Not Keely. She'd struggled with low self-esteem, the condition exacerbated when her body had developed earlier than other girls her age. She'd received instant attention from older boys with impure motives. She knew that now, as she looked back on those days with the eyes of a woman.

Ethan hadn't treated her as his equal back then.

But he hadn't been cruel, either. He'd shown her genuine respect and had looked out for her when others had only wanted to cause her harm. And... and...

No, oh, Lord, no. Not him, not now.

Keely's face drained of color as the truth settled over her. She was falling in love with Ethan. Maybe she was already there. Hope bloomed beneath the shock and panic, but she denied the emotion, fought for air. For several, long seconds she forced her mind to calm, her breathing to slow.

How had she let down her guard? *When* had she let it down?

Had it been that Sunday night he'd come over to her house to check on Felicity? Had it been sometime after, or perhaps even before? What did it matter?

Miserable, she stared at her unnaturally pale reflection. Her emotions were there, in her eyes, making them appear a bright, brilliant green. A dozen thoughts fluttered like hummingbird wings through her mind.

Ethan must not be allowed to know the change in her feelings for him. Tucking away her fears, she freshened up her makeup, fluffed her hair, then went in search of the man who'd battered down her defenses without her permission. Typical Ethan.

When she opened the door to him, he gave her a boyish grin and her stomach hit her toes.

Why did he have to be so good-looking? He

wore faded jeans and yet another T-shirt—Never Trust an Atom. They Make Up Everything—beneath the heavy coat he'd just unzipped.

"Good evening, Keely." Genuine affection threaded through the words. "Ready to take a walk through town?"

Unable to speak with her tongue stuck to the roof of her mouth, she smoothed a hand over her hair and simply nodded.

"Great. Let's go." He took her hand and guided her to his car.

Once they were in town, standing on the sidewalk that paralleled Main Street, she washed out her lungs with deep, calming breaths. The night was cold and clear and a paper-thin moon was visible above the mountain peaks. The buildings in town sparkled with thousands of tiny Christmas lights. The storefronts were decorated with garland, holly and wreaths. She breathed in again. This time the scent of pine filled her.

Proving he'd come prepared, Ethan dug into his pocket and whipped out a map with the parade route outlined in red. "I figure we can start our walk-through outside the Turkey Roost, since that's close to where the parade will begin."

"Works for me."

As he refolded the map, a gust of wind lifted hair off his forehead, revealing the granite-hard features that had become so dear to her. An odd feeling went through her, the kind of heady sensation that teenage girls got when they had a crush.

Get control of yourself. He's still the same big, bad, frustrating bane of your existence.

Keely attempted to smile, was pleased to see him return the gesture. Ethan Scott had an amazing smile. When she continued staring at him, he cocked an eyebrow and waited with a mock patience that sent her temper spiking.

"Go ahead," he urged. "I'm waiting."

"For what?"

"For the snarky comment. I can see it in your eyes. Let's have it, O'Toole." He leaned over her, his eyes glinting with familiar challenge. "Hit me with your best shot."

Her muscles went taut at the teasing note in his voice. And then a funny thing happened. She relaxed.

This was Ethan. *Her* Ethan, the man who came into her restaurant regularly. The man who calmed her fears over a sick child. The man who took her to the animal shelter, and then held her hand through the process of choosing just one.

"I've got nothing."

"Nothing? Give me a pen. I have to write this down."

A flash of affection swept across her soul, which she transformed into a smile. "Ha-ha."

His eyes went serious. Reaching up, he ran the

pad of his thumb across her cheek. "You're beautiful, Keely."

He'd never called her beautiful before, and because she saw the sincerity in his eyes, everything in her softened. "That's the first time you've ever said that to me."

"That can't be right. Are you sure?"

"Positive."

"Well, then." He dropped his hand. "I look forward to rectifying that gross injustice as often as possible."

"Oh, Ethan."

She no more conquered the emotion welling inside her when he draped his arm over her shoulders. "Come on, O'Toole. Let's check out the route, look for any potential snags, then, if you're really nice, I'll buy you dinner at Pizza Italiano."

"Sounds like a plan."

They fell into easy conversation as they walked the two-mile parade route through town.

Ethan told her about his college days and how tough it had been juggling school and work while also raising his three younger siblings. Keely told him about her job at the modeling agency and how she'd loved working in the business office so much she'd taken it upon herself to earn her business degree by attending night classes.

A light snowfall began as they drew near the parade's finish line. The good news was that they were less than a block north of Pizza Italiano. The restaurant was known for serving the best lasagna in Village Green.

Once again, Ethan issued his dinner invitation with the sincerity of a man asking a woman on a date.

Under the circumstances, with her emotions riding just below the surface, there was only one answer to the question. "Yes, Ethan, I would love to have dinner with you."

Pleased Keely had accepted his invitation, Ethan placed his hand on the small of her back and guided her across the street. With Christmas barely a week away, the crowd of holiday shoppers was thick on the sidewalks. People came and went from store to store, laughing and calling out to friends.

Carolers dressed in period costumes wove their way through the tangle of humanity, their voices lifted in perfect harmony as they sang the most popular songs of the season. The mood was festive, happy, and Ethan found himself humming along to "Silent Night." Keely joined him.

He took her hand, smiled into her sea-green eyes, then glanced up. The sky was midnight silk. The multitude of stars sparkled like diamonds on the black velvet backdrop. A blast of cold air managed to sneak under his collar.

Ethan reached around Keely, opened the door and waited for her to enter ahead of him. With her usual grace, she glided past him, head high, shoulders square. Her scent of lavender and wild orchid lingered in her wake, even as the unmistakable smells of tomato sauce and fresh-baked bread wafted on the air.

The place was busy, but there were still seats available. As they were led to a table for two, Ethan noticed how Keely's hair sparkled with melting snowflakes under the restaurant's lights. The woman fascinated him. This vivid awareness worried him, even as a wave of emotion washed through him.

There was a tenderness in him he'd experienced for only one other woman, a willingness to sacrifice his own needs for hers, to go the distance no matter the obstacles.

His shoulders felt heavy, as did his feet. A part of him was tired of fighting his attraction for Keely—his neighbor, his friend. Even as the thought formed, guilt whipped through him. Tracy's private memorial was in a few days and even though he had no plans to attend, Ethan's mind wasn't supposed to be on another woman.

Keely smiled at him from over her shoulder and he felt a portion of his burden lift. He'd said goodbye to Tracy. She'd want him to move on. Could he take another chance at love, knowing how precarious life was, how quickly he could lose everything? He shifted around Keely and pulled out her chair.

"Thank you," she whispered.

"My pleasure." Without thinking too hard about what he was doing, he leaned forward and pressed his hand over hers. "Hope you're hungry."

"Starving." She rotated her wrist until their palms were touching. For a brief moment, he saw his own tumultuous feelings reflected in her eyes.

Could they be more than—

Did they dare try to—

Cutting off each thought before it fully materialized, he rounded the table and took the chair facing Keely.

The waiter soon arrived and took their orders. Lasagna for them both.

As the waiter walked away, Keely smiled.

Ethan felt another burst of attraction, stronger than the one before. "I like you, Keely." He took her hand again. "More than I think you realize."

"I like you, too, Ethan." Her voice was wistful, wary. "I've enjoyed our time together these past few weeks, more than I thought possible."

He laughed at the grudging admission. "I don't know if you mean that as a compliment or an insult."

"Maybe a little of both." She pulled her hand free, cocked her head to the side as if she could see straight through the inside of his brain. "You do a good job of keeping people at a distance. For all the time we've spent together, I still don't feel as though I truly know you."

Picking at the tongs of his fork, he thought through her words, as if glimpsing himself for the first time from another's perspective. He saw a man alone, needing no one, seeking no one's help. The words from a long-ago sermon came to him. *Man is made to be in community.*

"You're right. I do keep others at a distance," he admitted for the first time in his life. "I have since my parents' car accident. From the moment I was forced to identify their bodies, I've always been the one others turn to for help."

"Who do you turn to?"

"No one."

"Sounds like a lonely existence."

His life was lonely. Or rather it had been, until Keely had called the house phone in a panic. Nothing had been the same since, and he wasn't entirely sorry for the change in his life.

"I suppose there is a certain loneliness in knowing that every decision I make carries a burden, and a consequence."

He felt the enormity of what he said crashing in on him. Even ignoring Phyllis's many calls held repercussions, not only for him but also for Tracy's mother, for her entire family. He was suddenly tired, the kind of exhaustion that couldn't be slept off.

"You aren't alone, Ethan." Keely's words came at him as if she were speaking to him from behind a wall of water. "You have your family. And you have…me."

He should have expected the declaration. He and Keely were friends now. Yet his pulse sped up. And he found himself speaking the truth in his heart. "You have me, too, Keely."

Something sad slid into her gaze. "Do I?"

"Yes, you do." The moment felt bigger than the words they were speaking.

"Oh, Ethan." She smiled, but a pensive light still lingered in her gaze. "I need to tell you something about my time in New York, I—"

Her phone buzzed, cutting her off midsentence. She glanced at the screen, lifted panic-stricken eyes to him. "It's Olivia."

"Answer it."

She lifted the phone to ear. "Olivia, what's wrong? Is it Felicity?"

Face grim, she listened to whatever his sister said in response to the question. "Oh. Oh, the poor thing."

She listened for several seconds longer, shared a worried look with Ethan. He could hear Olivia's muffled voice. Keely frowned. "Is she crying?"

More of the one-sided conversation passed. Then Keely said into the phone, "Tell her I'm on my way."

She ended the call and stuffed her phone back in her purse. "I have to go. Felicity's homesick."

"I'll drive you over to Olivia's." Before she could

argue, he held up a hand to stop her. "It's closer than taking you home."

"You don't mind?"

"Not at all." He motioned for the waiter, gave an abbreviated explanation and requested the check.

As he helped Keely into her coat, and escorted her out onto the sidewalk, he noticed her valiant attempt to ward off tears. "I can't help thinking this is my fault, that I pushed her too hard to make friends."

"Lots of children her age experience separation anxiety." He opened the car door, waited until she climbed in, then leaned his forearm on the roof. "This isn't abnormal behavior for a seven-year-old."

She let out a weighty sigh. "I hope you're right."

Taking a shortcut through town, he made it from the restaurant to Olivia's house in record time. He'd barely pulled his SUV to a stop when Keely dashed out of the car and up the front steps. By the time he entered the house, he was confronted with three sobbing little girls.

"Please don't hate me," Flicka wailed.

"We don't hate you," one of the twins said while the other rubbed her back and added, "We get homesick sometimes, too."

Their kindness seemed to make Flicka cry harder.

"If it's okay with Keely, you can come back

tomorrow afternoon," Olivia suggested. "And you can finish watching the movie with the girls then."

"I...I'd like that a lot." Her little voice trembled with a mixture of misery and tempered hope. Ethan's heart broke for the kid.

"Then that's what we'll do," Keely confirmed, pulling the child into a hug. "But for now, I think we all could use a good night's sleep. Things will look better in the morning."

Goodbyes were said, hugs were given, more tears flowed and then, finally, Ethan and Keely were back on the road with Flicka bundled up in the backseat. Her soft whimpers cut deep.

Having never been through anything quite like that before, Ethan was as emotionally wrung out as the little girl in his car. Parenting, he decided, especially parenting little girls, wasn't for sissies.

As Ethan pulled his SUV into her driveway, Keely glanced over her shoulder. Sometime during the ride home, exhaustion had caught up with Felicity. "She's sound asleep."

"Not surprising. She's had an exhausting evening." He turned off the engine and twirled the keys around his finger before stuffing them in his pocket. "I'll carry her inside."

The offer was both unexpected and greatly appreciated.

"That would be really helpful, thanks." She waited for him to pull the child into his arms before reaching in and gathering up Felicity's overnight bag.

They entered the house in silence, managing to get the child upstairs and in the bed without waking her. Grateful for his assistance, Keely walked Ethan to the front door. "Thank you for your help."

Shadows covered most of his face, but she was able to read the intent in his eyes a second before he gathered her close. Setting her head on his chest, she resisted the urge to cling.

"She's going to be okay, Keely. Even children from stable households get homesick."

"I pray you're right."

She could feel the rise and fall of his breathing beneath her cheek. The emotion of the evening was catching up with her and she didn't know what to do, what to say, so she just stood there, drawing on his strength.

Eventually, his hold loosened. Tenderly, with great care, he tucked a stray piece of hair behind her ear. "Call me if you need me to come back over."

"You don't have to do that."

"I'm here for you, Keely. You aren't in this alone. Okay?"

She nodded.

"Call me," he reiterated, in a soft, serious tone. No smile. No teasing banter.

This wasn't a game for him. Well, it wasn't for her, either. It was real and complicated and she thought she might cry, because she was in over her head. With Felicity. With Ethan. She'd never felt this out of control in her life.

"Good night, Keely." Taking her face in his hands, he kissed her gently on the lips and then he was gone, leaving her to gaze after his retreating back.

Mind reeling, she shut the door behind him, pressed her forehead to the wood and let the tears come, let them trail down her cheeks unfettered. She was falling in love with Ethan Scott, the big, bad, frustrating bane of her existence and one of the kindest men she knew.

Love was supposed to make her happy, wasn't it? Yet Keely had never been more miserable in her life.

Chapter Thirteen

Ethan was greeted at the back door by two tail-wagging, rowdy dogs, one of which had a shredded throw pillow clamped between his teeth. The other had the telltale signs of feathers clinging to his black fur.

Evidently, the dogs had thrown a party in his absence.

Torn between amusement and annoyance over the mess he now had to clean up, he pointed an accusing finger at the culprit holding the pillow in his mouth. "Looks like you killed it dead."

As if presenting a hard-earned trophy from an epic battle, Cupcake—they seriously needed to change the animal's name—dropped the pillow at Ethan's feet.

Giving into a laugh, he petted the puppy. "Good dog."

Baloo woofed softly to remind Ethan he had another animal in the house that required his attention. In the hopes of saving the rest of his pillows, he said, "Let's go for a walk."

Still dressed in his winter gear, Ethan snapped leashes into collars, then herded the dogs out the front door.

He steered the animals in the direction of Hawkins Park. The going was slow. Between the two of them, Baloo and Cupcake managed to sniff every bush and tree trunk on the block.

From the depths of Ethan's back pocket came the sound of his cell phone ringing. Gripping both leashes in one hand, he dug out the phone with his other. A quick look at the name on the screen and he let the call go to voice mail again.

He knew he was putting off the inevitable, but he didn't want to hear Tracy's mother continue to make her case for why he should attend the private memorial ceremony.

Back at the house, as he refilled the dogs' water bowls, conscience got the better of him. He pulled out his cell phone again. There were nine missed calls, all from the same South Carolina number. Giving in, he scrolled to the oldest and waited for the inevitable plea.

"Ethan, this is Phyllis again. Please call me. I want to discuss the particulars of Tracy's memorial service with you."

He hit the delete button.

The next two messages were variations of the first, each one making a case for Ethan to attend a ceremony that included scattering Tracy's ashes over her favorite lake. *Delete.*

Phyllis eventually quit identifying herself, preferring instead to get straight to the point. "Ethan, you have to come to the memorial. Tracy was as much yours as she was ours. She would want—"

Delete.

There was no reason to listen to the rest of the messages. He knew what Mrs. Jenkins wanted from him. He would eventually call her back, but not tonight, not until he had his argument for turning down her request formulated in his mind.

Sinking onto the couch, he closed his eyes and desperately tried to call up Tracy's image. Her features weren't crystal clear anymore and that felt like the biggest betrayal of all.

Abruptly, he rose, went to the bookshelf in the study off the den. He fished around until he found the professionally made photo album her mother had sent him a month after the funeral. Taking the book with him, he returned to the living room.

The dogs sat at his feet, looking at him with adoring eyes. He dropped a hand to each of their heads, heaved a tight breath.

He felt empty inside. The sorrow was there, but so was a healthy dose of annoyance. He'd said goodbye to Tracy at her military funeral. He'd come home and built a new life for himself, away from the military, away from the memories.

He'd surrounded himself with the familiar, yet

had remained distant from the ones he loved most. It had been easier that way, not getting too involved, not stepping out on faith. Simply existing.

Feeling as frozen inside as the snow on the ground, Ethan opened the album, placed his finger on a picture of him and Tracy. His hand shook violently on the page as the weight of grief overwhelmed him.

"I can't do this right now." He tossed the book of photos on top of the coffee table.

Picking up the remote, he flicked on the television and settled in to watch whatever football game he could find. His goal was simple, to numb his pain, to forget.

To focus on anything but the woman he'd lost and the life that had almost been his.

At twenty minutes to nine on Sunday morning, Keely sent Felicity upstairs to brush her teeth and took the opportunity to call Ethan. She told herself she simply wanted to inform him that Felicity was feeling better and actually wanted to go to church this morning. But that wasn't entirely true. Keely also wanted to make sure they were still…what?

Friends? Something more?

Mildly annoyed with herself, she keyed in his number.

He answered on the third ring. "Good morning, Keely."

Was he pleased to hear from her? She couldn't tell by his neutral tone.

"Hey," she said in a breezy voice, all cool and casual. "I wanted to let you know Felicity's better this morning."

"That's a relief."

"In fact, she and I will be leaving for church in five minutes."

"She's good with that?"

"It was her idea. Anyway, I'm telling you this in case you want to let the dogs out while we're gone."

"Ah."

Biting down on her lower lip, she glanced out the kitchen window, wondered if Ethan was also in his kitchen, looking out in her direction. "You wouldn't want to come to church with us, would you?"

A long, tense silence met the question.

"Ethan?"

"I'd planned to start putting up the Christmas lights on your house this morning."

"Oh," she said, her breath rattling in her throat.

The man was just being neighborly, following through on an earlier promise. Except…she could feel her pulse picking up speed. And last night, even before they'd picked up Felicity, she and Ethan had crossed some sort of invisible line.

If she closed her eyes she could see him on a ladder, wearing one of his sardonic T-shirts while he strung lights along her roofline. Another scene flitted across her mind, replacing the first. She and Ethan were sitting by the fire in her hearth, a dark-haired toddler or two playing at their feet, a couple of dogs snoozing away and a—

Whoa. She'd been barely on speaking terms with the man two weeks ago. Thinking in terms of anything beyond friendship was getting way ahead of herself.

"Thanks. I'll leave the garage door open. The lights are in the large box next to the tool kit. Should be easy enough to find what you need."

"I'll figure it out." A short pause followed the remark. "Will I see you and Flicka later this afternoon at my sister's?"

Even before they'd married, Connor and Olivia had started a tradition of feeding family and friends every Sunday afternoon. They lived in a rambling old house on the edge of town that had once been an orphanage—of sorts—in the Old West for children born to prostitutes.

The Scotts and Mitchells had direct connections to Charity House. So did Keely's family, as well as half a dozen others in town. "Felicity and I have plans to head over after church."

"I'm bringing Baloo with me, but Cupcake has to stay behind for obvious reasons."

Keely hated that the puppy had to be left at Ethan's, but it couldn't be helped. She didn't want to spoil Felicity's surprise. "Poor little guy."

"Speaking of the poor little guy, I really have to insist on an immediate name change, especially now that he's bunking with us Scott men."

"What? Cupcake's not masculine enough for you?"

Ethan's derisive snort was answer enough. "From now on, I'm calling him…" He paused as if contemplating various possibilities. "…Tank. Has a nice ring to it, don't you think? Says I'm tough, don't mess with me."

She bit back a laugh. "No, not Tank."

"Okay, how about…T-bone?"

She kind of liked that one, but it wasn't up to her. Or Ethan, for that matter. The dog was Felicity's Christmas gift. "Not T-bone, either."

"Axel, Spike, Razor Blade?"

"No, no and definitely not."

"Come on, Keely, work with me here."

She switched the phone to her other ear, lowered her voice to a whisper. "I thought we agreed to let Felicity decide."

"Right, muddy the waters with logic."

Her heart stuttered at the amused response and she admitted she'd lost objectivity. She'd let down her guard and Ethan had slipped beneath her defenses.

"Geronimo, Hank, Rawhide?"

"I'm hanging up now." She disconnected the call on his deep chuckle.

Moments later, Felicity entered the kitchen,

dressed and ready for church. "Molly and Megan promised to sit with me at Sunday school this morning. They really aren't mad I left last night. They both said so on the phone just now."

Keely made a mental note to buy those sweet girls each a very special Christmas present this year. "Well, then, we certainly don't want to be late."

It took three go-rounds for Keely to find an empty space in the crowded church parking lot. She dropped Felicity off in the second grade Sunday-school room, put her phone on vibrate and then entered the main sanctuary.

From a pew near the back, Olivia waved at her over. "Connor and I saved you a seat."

"Thanks."

She smiled. "Felicity's feeling better this morning," she told both her friends.

"I'm glad," they said in unison just as the worship band kicked off the first song.

With Christmas a week away, the sermon was on the power of God's love given in the form of His Son. "We haven't done a thing to earn this gift, freely given."

The young preacher paused, glanced over the congregation, making eye contact with several people, Keely one of them. "All we have to do is receive. Not easy, especially when we're also taught that it's better to give than receive." He paused again. "But if we don't first receive God's gift, we will have little to give others when the time comes."

The message resonated with Keely. She thought back over the year since she'd come home. She'd arrived with a shattered heart. She'd buried her pain with activity, working hard at the restaurant, volunteering at the church and around town.

She'd given her time, but not herself. She'd kept busy serving others, but never stopped long enough to receive back from them. Because receiving required vulnerability, and opening herself up to another heartache. She'd allowed Cutter's inability to let go of his past to keep her from claiming a future for herself.

How was she supposed to guide Felicity to live a healthy, functional life if she didn't model it herself?

"Keely." Olivia's hand touched her arm. "Are you okay?"

Opening her eyes, she smiled at her friend. "Yes, of course. I'm fine."

She wasn't, not really. But she would be, after she made some changes in her life. She would do it for Felicity. And maybe even for herself. She thought of her mother's favorite saying, *Begin as you mean to go.*

The sermon came to an end and Keely bowed her head for the closing prayer. She discovered during the announcements that the men's ministry was putting on a father/daughter dance Wednesday night in place of youth group.

Her first thought was of Felicity. Would she want to attend? Probably, especially if the Mitchell twins were going with their father. Who would take Felicity?

Ethan came immediately to mind, but Keely couldn't see herself asking him. There was another option. Her brother.

Then why didn't that feel right?

Why, when she shut her eyes, could Keely only picture Ethan escorting Felicity to the father/daughter dance?

Chapter Fourteen

With Baloo riding shotgun, Ethan arrived at Connor and Olivia's place just after noon. Pulling his SUV in behind Keely's Jeep, he studied the gigantic, newly renovated house. There was history here, family history for the Scotts and the Mitchells and several others in town. Ethan was pleased that the brick and stone structure still had an old-fashioned charm that spoke of days gone by.

He cut the engine, noted the number of cars already in the drive. Ready to eat, Ethan snapped Baloo's leash into his collar, then let the dog out of the car. Ryder's pickup pulled to a stop behind Ethan's SUV.

Still dressed in scrubs, his brother hopped out of the truck, stretched his long legs as if working out invisible kinks. His face held signs of a stressful night in the ER.

"You just getting off work?"

"There was a bad accident out on the highway

just as my shift was ending. I stuck around to help out. Hey, boy." Yawning, Ryder leaned down and gave Baloo's head a good scrubbing. "Hope Liv made extra mashed potatoes. I'm in the mood for some serious carbs."

After a cursory knock on the front door, two men and a dog entered the house to the sound of organized chaos. Children's laughter mingled with adult conversations, the clinking of dinnerware accompanied a popular Christmas song wafting on the air from invisible speakers built into the wall. People milled about with plates overflowing with food.

"I see dinner is served." A grin slid across Ryder's face.

Ethan gave him a fist bump. Announcing their arrival, Baloo let out a single, loud *woof.*

The Mitchells' dog, a fat-bellied pug-and-beagle mix, came wheeling around the corner at warp speed. The two dogs greeted each other with the familiarity of old friends.

"Well, well. Look who the dogs dragged in." Dressed in jeans and a cable-knit sweater, Connor joined them in the hallway. "Hope you came hungry."

"Need you ask?"

Laughing at Ryder's question, Connor led them into the dining room where an elaborate buffet was set up. "We're informal today. Fill a plate and sit wherever you like."

"On it." Ryder made a beeline for the food.

Ethan hung back, taking in the eclectic mix of people already assembled. He'd known everyone in the room since grade school. Nodding at familiar faces, he circled his gaze around the room, checking for two people in particular.

"Last time I checked, Keely and Felicity were in the kitchen helping Olivia and the girls."

"Who said I was looking for Keely and Flicka?"

"Weren't you?" Connor's voice held no small amount of irony. "My mistake."

Deciding there was no good response, not without opening up another conversation about the way he was living his life, Ethan moved toward the food table.

Ham, thickly sliced tenderloin and several other kinds of meat shared space with a dozen side dishes, including Ryder's hoped-for mashed potatoes. Another, smaller table in the corner held desserts, one of which was Ethan's favorite, pecan pie.

Connor clapped him on the back. "Have at it, my friend."

"Don't have to tell me twice." He picked up a plate and began moving counterclockwise around the table. He nodded to Keely's twin brother, who was working his way around in the opposite direction.

Beau O'Toole was the polar opposite of his hardworking, serious sister and the quintessential poster boy for Colorado ski country. The man's startling green eyes were identical to Keely's, but where her hair was a fiery red, Beau's was a sun-tipped bronze.

They met up at the plate of ham.

Ethan eyed the man, noticed the signs of strain on his face, the kind that came from battling physical pain. "You haven't been in the office for weeks. How's the shoulder?"

"Fine." The one-word answer came out clipped and irritated, belying the easygoing stance and overly casual tone.

Ethan took another inventory of the guy, this time with the eyes of a doctor. Beau filled his plate with his left hand. Telling. The former world champion was right-handed. The shoulder wasn't fine. "Make an appointment, Beau."

"My shoulder is good, Ethan. Let it go."

Not going to happen. When they'd gone skiing last week, Beau had tackled the slopes with unusual aggression. He was clearly paying the price now. "Still doing your rehab exercises?"

Darkness filled Beau's gaze. "No point. My career's over."

"Competitively speaking, but it doesn't mean you can't ski for fun and go as hard at it as you did last weekend and—"

Beau cut him off. "I'll make an appointment if you'll stop talking."

"My job here is done."

"Excellent." Beau finished filling his plate.

As he left the room, Ethan fell into step beside him. Muttering something about pushy friends, Beau broke off toward the living room. Ethan slowed his steps, debating whether to follow. He'd made his point.

As he hovered in the doorway, he watched Flicka in an animated discussion with Connor's twins, something about a dance later that week.

Ethan's first instinct was to turn and walk away. He had good reason to put distance between him and the kid. She'd made it clear she wanted a father, with a look in her eyes that warned Ethan he was at the top of her list. It wouldn't be fair to let her spin hopes and dreams around him, as if it was possible he could fill that role in her life.

"I can't go to the dance," Flicka said, her voice small and vulnerable, her head hung low. "I don't have a father."

Molly patted her on the back with an obvious show of sympathy. "My daddy is taking both my sister and me, I'm sure he'll take you, too."

Flicka lifted her head. "You really think so?"

"I don't see why not."

Ethan struggled with a vortex of emotions, sadness, remorse, a yearning to provide the little girl with something real and lasting, something that went far beyond a dance at the church. His soul was being ripped to shreds. This was the type of pain he'd been avoiding since Tracy's death, for good reason.

Seeking escape, he melted into the shadows, found an empty chair in the hallway. He set his untouched plate on the small table beside him and shut his eyes. He regretted the move.

He was back in Tracy's apartment, early in their relationship, wearing the tux he'd bought for the father/daughter dance at Fort Bragg Army post. Tracy's daughter, Samantha, was beaming up at him with the adoration of a daughter. The memory was fresh, and too, too real, as if the dance had been just yesterday, rather than two years ago.

Something inside him broke.

He couldn't breathe, couldn't think, couldn't stay in this chair, in this house, another second.

Blinking open his eyes, he reminded himself that what he'd lost could never be recovered. Tracy was dead. Samantha was living with her biological father. Ethan was probably only a distant memory to the little girl.

Grief came hot and fast, clawing at him.

He needed air—now. He abruptly rose, left the hallway with clipped, purposeful strides.

Someone called his name.

He kept walking, not stopping until he was outside in the backyard, bent at the waist, drawing in large gulps of air. He blamed his reaction on Flicka's desire for a father, but that wasn't the full truth. He'd had Tracy and Samantha on his mind ever since he listened to Mrs. Jenkins's voice mail yesterday.

Everything he'd put behind him gnawed at his composure with fresh vigor.

"Ethan?" Keely's voice was soft, so soft it almost wasn't there, like a whisper in his head.

"Ethan." Her hand touched his sleeve. "Talk to me. Are you ill?"

He took a shuddering breath, continuing the process until the fire in his chest eased and the air didn't catch in his throat. "I..." He swallowed, once, twice. "I'm good now."

"No, you're not."

Two more breaths, a slow blink, and he was feeling calmer.

Keely moved her hand down his arm, clasped her fingers with his. "You were caught in a panic attack."

He nodded, surprised at the relief the silent admission brought him. He'd kept the past locked inside him for so long, ignoring it, pretending all was well. It was a relief to admit that the pain was still with him.

"Did something happen in Afghanistan, something you've never shared with anyone?"

The question brought him up short. She thought he was suffering from PTSD?

"I'm okay, Keely." He pulled their joined hands to rest against his heart, the rhythm steadier for the connection. "I just needed some air."

She studied his face for several long moments.

"Will you tell me what happened to make you run outside, away from your family and friends?"

He recognized the concern in her eyes and desperately wanted to share his past with her. The words were there in his mind, struggling for release, but they stalled halfway up his throat. "I'm sorry, Keely. I…can't."

Not yet.

But in that moment he knew Connor was right. Ethan needed to start living again. He needed to make peace with Tracy's death. He would eventually tell Keely everything about his life with Tracy. It was the right thing to do, the only thing to do.

The realization brought a new level of calm. Finally, he was able to breathe easier. Something came and went in her eyes, something that looked like sadness, with a twinge of disappointment, maybe even pity.

Pity was the last thing he wanted from her.

What do *you want?*

Ethan didn't know. All he knew was that this woman was in his mind, maybe even his heart. Living again would somehow involve her.

How had he let this happen? How had he allowed another woman and her child slip past his guard?

Even knowing the danger, he felt affection awaken in his chest. Affection for Keely. He didn't want that, not here, not now. Or maybe he did, maybe he needed to feel something again. And maybe Keely was just the woman—

No.

He hadn't fully let Tracy go. He knew that now, confirmed by his inability to stop thinking about her since her mother's phone calls.

Instead of exploring the complicated feelings racing through him, Ethan changed the subject. "Have you ever made ice cream from snow?"

Keely blinked at the startling shift in topic. Standing before her, his gaze dark and turbulent, Ethan Scott stole her breath. He looked so vulnerable. Regretful and sad.

Longing to erase his pain, she lifted her hand to his face.

He stepped out of reach.

"Well?" He tilted his head to one side. "Have you ever made snow ice cream?"

Her heart started beating out of control. She was sure he heard it. Unable to look directly into his eyes, she lowered her gaze and concentrated on the slogan on his T-shirt. If Things Get Any Worse, I'll Have to Ask You to Stop Helping.

Message received.

And yet everything had just gotten a whole lot more complicated. Keely couldn't stay detached any longer. She couldn't pretend indifference, or a lack of caring. Ever since Cutter, pushing others away had been her modus operandi. Now she was the one being pushed away.

"I get it, Ethan. You don't want to talk about whatever is bothering you."

His eyes went flat.

Wonderful, she'd made him angry. "I'm sorry. I'll leave you alone with your thoughts."

She made to leave.

He caught her by the arm. "Don't go."

The emotion in those two simple words hovered on the air between them. Ethan's pain was so real, so thick, Keely nearly choked on it.

Somewhere overhead, a plane crossed the sky. She looked up at the clear, brittle blue, but found no inspiration to help her break through his barriers. "You don't have to tell me—"

"I want to, Keely, but not here, not yet, not today."

An unspoken promise hung in his words. He would eventually tell her what was weighing so heavy on his heart. She should be relieved. She felt only despair. She'd heard similar words from Cutter two weeks before he retracted his marriage proposal.

Only in hindsight, as she'd reviewed their relationship with a fresh perspective, had Keely recognized the signs of a man still pining for his dead wife.

Ethan had those same signs now.

She thought she might cry. "When you're ready, then."

He nodded, clearly relieved she let the matter drop. "What do you know about the father/daughter dance at the church?"

The lack of transition to the new topic dragged a gasp from her. Had Felicity asked him to take her? It would certainly explain the wariness she detected in his stance, the pinched expression on his face.

She gathered her racing thoughts. "The dance is this Wednesday night, given by the men's ministry at our church. They've scheduled it in place of regular youth group. It's a Christmas theme, of course."

"Is there an age limit for the kids attending?"

"I don't believe so. I heard Mr. Larson telling Pastor Rick that he's taking his daughter again this year." She couldn't help grinning. Abe Larson had recently turned ninety-eight and his daughter Alma was well into her seventies.

Ethan finally cracked a smile. "Do you think your brother will take Flicka?"

"Probably." Why was Ethan asking so many questions? "Do you know something I don't? Something to do with the dance?"

Looking uncomfortable, he rubbed a hand

across his jaw. "I'm pretty sure Flicka wants to go. I overheard her telling the twins."

With this new piece of information, Keely would definitely be bringing up the topic with her brother.

"There's more."

Keely didn't like what she heard in Ethan's voice. "All right."

"When Flicka and I were out shopping yesterday, I asked her what she wanted for Christmas."

Dread took up residence in Keely's heart. "What did she say?"

"A father."

Poor, dear, sweet Felicity. Her mother was in prison; she was living in a strange town, starting a new school and spending Christmas with people she hardly knew. Her one and only wish? A father. And she'd shared that information with Ethan. It didn't take a psychology degree to figure out why.

"That had to have been awkward for you."

"You have no idea."

"How did you respond?"

"I told her it was pretty short notice and it would be difficult to find her a father this year."

"That's certainly true."

"She seemed a little disappointed, but I think she expected my response. I then asked her if there was anything else on her list." He shifted his stance, stuffed his hands in his pockets. "She said a puppy."

Keely wanted to break out in song. "Well, that's something."

"Bruiser is going to be a big hit Christmas morning."

"You mean Cupcake."

"Bullet?"

Keely's lips twitched at his hopeful expression. *"Cupcake."*

"Maximus?"

She was laughing now, and so was he. Ethan Scott was frustrating, annoying, with far too many secrets swimming in his eyes, but Keely was starting to like him, in a way that had nothing to do with friendship.

"Cupcake, and that's the end of it."

Silence fell over them.

At least the mood was lighter now. For that, Keely was grateful. She still wanted to know what had set Ethan off. Had it been talk of the father/ daughter dance? She didn't think so.

There was so much she didn't know about the man, so many missing pieces.

He bent down, scooped up a handful of snow and studied it with quiet fervor. "Since you have evaded my question twice, I'm going to assume you've never made snow ice cream."

Hands twisted at her waist, she concentrated on the snow nestled in his palm. She could feel his gaze on her, watching her closely. "Your assumption would be correct."

"It's time for a cooking lesson, Ms. O'Toole." He dumped the snow back on the ground.

"By all means, Dr. Scott, educate me."

They were in the kitchen, deep in the middle of her cooking lesson, when Beau entered the room. "Hey, sis, came to say goodbye."

Ryder was one step behind him, suffocating a yawn behind his hand. "I'm heading out, too."

Both men's gazes landed on the colorful candy sprinkles Ethan had set on the counter.

Proving he still had the sweet tooth of a ten-year-old boy, Beau's eyebrows shot up. "Are we about to miss something good?"

"Not good. Great." With one hand holding a bottle of vanilla extract and the other reaching for a bag of sugar, Ethan tossed a negligent glance over his shoulder. "I'm teaching Keely how to make snow ice cream, thereby completing her culinary education."

Moving deeper in the room, Ryder gaped at his brother. "Since when do you know how to do anything in the kitchen more complicated than ordering takeout?"

Giving a dismissive snort, Ethan spread the ingredients out on the counter. "All I need is fresh snow and a whisk."

"You know how to use a whisk?" Beau looked duly impressed.

"I'm not a complete Neanderthal."

Ryder peered at the ingredients scattered across the counter. "Snow ice cream is a kid's treat. Where did you learn how to make—" He cut his own words off, winced. "I mean…ah, man. I didn't mean to bring up a sore subject. I—"

"Shut up, Ryder." Ethan growled the words.

"Shutting up. Shutting up right now." Palms raised, Ryder backpedaled toward the door he'd previously come from.

Keely looked from one Scott brother to the other. Unease had fallen over the entire room. Even Beau looked uncomfortable.

What was she missing?

Felicity and the Mitchell twins rushed into the room. Molly spoke for the group. "Daddy says you're making snow ice cream. We've come to help."

Chapter Fifteen

Snow ice cream was a huge success. Not long after the last batch was served, a mass exodus from Olivia and Connor's house began.

Keely had promised Felicity they would shop for their Christmas tree that very afternoon, but she needed to speak with her brother first. She caught up with him in the foyer.

"Can you stop by the restaurant and make sure Sylvia put today's receipts in the safe?" Keely trusted her manager, but the Sunday lunch crowd was heavy during the holidays and she'd feel more comfortable knowing for certain that the money was locked up. "I could do it myself, but it's out of my way."

"No problem." He jammed a ski cap on his head. "I was heading in that direction anyway."

Squinting in the darkened hallway, she assessed her brother, her *twin* brother, wondering why their connection wasn't as strong as it had been when they were younger. As kids, they'd been close, practically able to read each other's minds. The link had continued into adulthood.

But lately, whenever Keely looked in brother's eyes, she saw a stranger. He'd been different since moving back to Village Green, still her brother and yet…not. She blamed the gulf partly on herself. She hadn't taken the time to reach out enough. It was another unfortunate consequence of Cutter's change of heart, another circumstance of allowing his past to influence her future.

"Felicity and I are picking out a Christmas tree this afternoon. Want to come over later and help us decorate it?"

"Sorry, I have plans."

Keely sighed. Her brother hadn't even attempted to come up with a plausible excuse. Though she desperately wanted to press for details, she didn't dare. Not when a potential audience could enter the foyer at any minute.

Beau turned to go, then swung back around. "I meant to tell you earlier, but I got distracted by ice cream."

She laughed. "Understandable."

"Yeah, well, Felicity mentioned the father/ daughter dance Wednesday night. I'd be happy to take her." He sounded sincere.

It was nice of Beau to offer, and yet Keely had really hoped Ethan would step in. She knew it wasn't fair to expect that of him. He was only their neighbor, and probably still reeling from his "daddy" conversation with the little girl.

Since Beau was family, there wouldn't be any expectations beyond the event. "The dance is formal."

Annoyance whipped across his face. "I own a suit."

"*And* a tie?"

"The tie could be a problem," he muttered.

She started to say something snarky about him being the quintessential ski bum, but the sound of footsteps had her holding her tongue.

"I can loan you one." Ethan's voice came from behind her.

Keely spun around.

"Don't look so surprised, O'Toole. I own nice clothes."

"I can get my own tie," Beau growled at him.

Ethan lifted empty hands in the universal show of surrender. "Just making a friendly offer to save you time and unnecessary hassle."

"Thanks, but I'm good."

An odd strain fell over the two men. It grew thicker when Ethan drew alongside Keely, putting them shoulder-to-shoulder.

Beau's eyes narrowed. He shifted his gaze to Keely, then back to Ethan.

Something passed between the two. Keely wasn't sure what, only that it was not a pleasant meeting of the minds. There seemed to be more going on between them than the issue of a tie.

"Walk outside with me," Beau asked Ethan, not Keely. "I have something I want to run by you."

"All right." Ethan whistled for Baloo, who appeared seconds later in the hallway, tail wagging. With his hand on the dog's collar, he made a deliberate show of giving Keely his undivided attention. "I'll see you later?"

"Sure."

Beau gave her a brief nod and then stepped outside with Ethan, Baloo following behind him. As she watched, Keely couldn't tell what they were discussing, but it seemed serious.

At least Felicity would be attending the father/daughter dance at the church with Beau. Keely clung to that happy thought as she went in search of the little girl. She found her playing a board game with Molly and Megan on the living room floor.

For a moment, Keely watched Felicity. She appeared comfortable, animated and fully in the moment, a sure sign she was over whatever had made her homesick last night.

Deciding to give her a bit more time with her friends, Keely slipped out of the doorway and moved into the kitchen, where Olivia was stacking plates in the dishwasher. "What can I do to help?"

"Not a thing." Olivia smiled at her from over her shoulder. "Connor and I are nearly finished."

Her husband entered the kitchen from the dining room, set several empty bowls in the sink. "This is the last of them."

"Splendid."

Grinning, Connor moved in behind his wife, wrapped his arms around her waist. "You are a treasure, Mrs. Mitchell. Have I told you how much I love you?"

Olivia sighed against him. "Not in the last half hour."

"A terrible oversight." Seeming not to care that Olivia's hands were wet and full of soapsuds, Connor whipped her around to face him, then waltzed her through the kitchen, humming a tune from another time.

As she matched her husband step for step, Olivia smiled up at Connor with such love in her eyes Keely felt a moment of pure envy. *I want that, Lord. I want to love and be loved without reservation, without conditions, without someone from the past standing between us.*

She thought she'd found it with Cutter. The widower had said all the right words, made all the right promises. When he spoke of his dead wife, he'd been reverent and wistful, but had assured Keely he was over the loss of her.

Keely had made the assumption that the joy he'd found in his first marriage was a sign that he knew how to love, how to commit totally to a relationship.

What neither of them had understood at the time

was that his heart still belonged to his dead wife. Tragically, he'd only accepted the truth *after* he gave Keely an engagement ring.

The retraction of his marriage proposal had been painful for them both. Keely actually felt sorry for Cutter. He would never truly be able to live a full life until he was able to let go of his wife. Keely hoped he could find the courage to do so. He deserved to be free, to find happiness.

But then, so did she.

The next time she gave her heart to a man, he would not be pining for the woman he'd lost.

Connor swept Olivia into a deep dip, then bent over and kissed her square on the mouth. They both came up laughing and smiling into each other's eyes, as if the world had slipped away, leaving only the two of them. Olivia was Connor's second chance at love. Keely took hope in that.

"I love you," he whispered to his wife.

"Oh, Connor, I love you, too."

Feeling as though she was intruding on a private moment, Keely silently slipped from the room.

Felicity met her in the hallway. "The game's over. Molly won, but I'll get her next time."

"I'm sure you will." She ran her hand over the little girl's head. "Ready to go pick out our Christmas tree?"

"Yes, please."

They were soon on the road, heading to the north end of town. Everyone in Village Green knew that the best trees were sold at the tree lot managed by the coaches from the local high school.

Keely pulled into the lot and smiled at the extensive inventory still available. As she unbuckled her seat belt, Felicity informed Keely that, "Dr. Ethan told me we should get a Colorado blue spruce, or nothing at all."

Sounded like something he would say. Hiding a smile behind a cough, Keely met her cousin at the front of the Jeep. "Well, then, let's hope they have an assortment of blue spruces to choose from."

"They have to be *Colorado* blue spruces."

"Of course."

With help from John Weston, the football coach and one of Keely's former classmates, they located the perfect tree. It was nearly seven feet tall, with full branches, a straight trunk and no bald spots. It was also a Colorado blue spruce.

"For an additional ten dollars," John informed her, "we'll deliver the tree within the next twenty-four hours."

"Done." She paid for the tree and delivery in cash.

On the way home they stopped at a store that carried children's clothing and picked out a new dress for Felicity to wear to the father/daughter dance.

At home they discovered two surprises. The first was Ethan on a ladder, hanging outdoor twinkle lights. The other was their Christmas tree perched against the front porch.

"You ladies have excellent timing." Ethan waved at them from his perch near the edge of the roof. "I'm nearly done."

He looped the string of lights around a hook connected to the overhang. He then stuffed some sort of manly looking tool in his back pocket and climbed down the ladder.

Though it was barely dusk, the sky a pretty purple-gray, he suggested they checked out his day's work. He fiddled with the timer a moment, and then plugged the main cord into an outdoor socket.

The house burst into light.

"It's wonderful," Keely breathed in pure delight.

Felicity responded with more enthusiasm, clapping her hands while also singing the chorus of "Jingle Bells" at the top of her lungs. Smiling over the child's head, Ethan and Keely joined in.

It was a perfect moment, full of joy and hope and everything good about the Christmas season.

Eyes less distant than they'd been this afternoon, Ethan jerked a nod toward the house. "I see you followed my recommendation."

Not sure what he meant, Keely angled her head. "How so?"

"The tree." He clasped her shoulders and turned her toward the front of her house. "That is most definitely a Colorado blue spruce."

She laughed.

He shoved his hands in his pockets. "Need help getting it inside?"

Wiggling her recently manicured fingernails, she gave him a droll eyebrow lift. "What do you think?"

"I think…" He made a grand show of studying her outstretched hands. "You are a girly girl."

"I'll take that as a compliment."

"What about me?" Felicity scooted between them so she could gain Ethan's attention. "Am I a girly girl, too?"

"You, my dear Flicka." He ruffled the child's blond curls. "Are the girly girliest of them all."

Ethan wrestled the tree inside Keely's house, careful not to bump the walls or leave too many pine needles on the floor. He was pleased to discover that while he'd been outside securing a stand to the tree's trunk, Keely and Flicka had been busy clearing away furniture in front of the large picture window that faced the street.

He set the tree in the now empty spot, then moved it around until Keely was satisfied with its position.

Stepping back, he removed his gloves, and studied the overall effect. "You made a good choice," he declared.

Flicka added her agreement.

Keely simply nodded. "Coach Weston assured

me this was the best Colorado blue spruce on the lot."

At the mention of the high school football coach, Ethan felt a spurt of irritation. Odd. He liked John Weston. Everyone in town liked him, especially women. The guy was young, single and, by all accounts, a man of integrity.

Had the football coach hit on Keely?

Something churned inside Ethan, something directly related to the smiling woman standing beside him. Each moment in her company made him feel alive, like he was finally home.

This afternoon, when her brother had point-blank asked him if he had his eye on Keely, romantically, Ethan hadn't said yes. But he hadn't said no, either. Instead he'd swiftly changed the subject, insisting the guy come into the office so Ethan could check his shoulder properly.

And that had sufficiently ended their conversation.

There was no denying Ethan had feelings for Keely. But what was he going to do about them?

"Okay, Keely. Are you in the white-lights-only camp or do you prefer colored lights? Think hard before you respond." He swiveled his head toward hers. "There is only one right answer."

With her expression giving nothing away, she reached inside a plastic bin and pulled out a string of lights. Hiding the bulbs from his gaze, she walked over to an outlet, plugged in the strand and an assortment of bright colors sparkled at her feet.

"We can now remain friends."

Laughing, she made a grand show of wiping off her forehead with the back of her hand. "Phew."

Flicka, already rummaging through another plastic bin, grabbed a box of ornaments. "Are you going to stay and help us decorate the tree?" she asked him.

The last time he'd decorated a tree had been with Tracy and Samantha. He didn't want the past encroaching on the present. He'd had enough of that for one day. He wanted to live in the moment, with Keely and Flicka.

But if he spent more time in their company, it would be that much harder to pull away after the holidays. He couldn't give either of them what they needed, though a part of him wished he could.

Perhaps he should leave now, before he got in too deep. He was working up an excuse when Flicka offered him a box of shiny red and gold ornaments.

"You can put these on the tree while I string the popcorn Keely and I made last night." Her eyes were full of little-girl innocence. How was he supposed to say no to that look?

Before he could stop himself, he was reaching for the box and saying, "Works for me."

Despite his concerns, the next two hours were pleasant. The three of them worked well together.

When the last ornament was hung, they stepped back as a single unit.

"It's the best tree ever," Flicka declared with no small amount of pride.

Ethan eyed the massive amounts of lights and twice as many ornaments. The result should have looked overdone and chaotic. Yet, somehow, with its mix of old-fashioned and modern bulbs, store-bought and homemade ornaments, the tree actually worked. "It does have something special about it."

Caught in the moment, Ethan found himself accepting Keely's invitation to stay for leftovers and cake.

"But I need to feed the…" He paused, barely stopping before he gave away Flicka's Christmas surprise. "…Baloo, first. Then I'll come back over."

Giggling, Felicity pressed a hand to her lips. "Is that what you call him now? *The* Baloo?"

The kid missed nothing. "He's only *the* Baloo on Sundays."

"That's just silly." She lowered her hand. "Can I come with you and help you feed *the* Baloo."

Keely came to his rescue. "Actually, little miss, you need to set the table."

The girl grumbled, but at Keely's reminder the task was one of her daily chores, she didn't argue further.

Dinner went well, as it had gone every other night Ethan dined with Keely and Flicka. The three of them were sliding into a nice rhythm. In fact, Ethan felt so comfortable that he didn't balk even when the kid invited him to stay for another movie night, *The Muppet Christmas Carol.*

Thus, he found himself sticking around until nine o'clock.

As the final credits rolled across the screen, Keely announced it was bedtime for Flicka, since she had school in the morning. "Two more days and it'll be Christmas break."

The child hopped to her feet and looked directly at Ethan with big, round, hopeful eyes. "Will you say bedtime prayers with me tonight?"

A tide of panic washed through his beleaguered soul. Yet no excuse came to mind.

"We can say them right here in the living room, because God hears us wherever we pray."

Consumed with indecision, Ethan shared a look with Keely. Her eyes had gone watery with emotion. The sight made him feel all kinds of things he hadn't felt in a year and a half.

He reached out and briefly touched her hand. "Okay." He turned back to Flicka. "We'll pray right here."

The kid wiggled onto the sofa between him and Keely. Squeezing her hands tightly together, she shut her eyes and rested her forehead on her knuckles.

Feeling as if he were coming apart from the inside out, Ethan adopted the same pose.

"Dear God," Flicka whispered, "please take care of my mommy in prison and let her know I'm okay living with Keely and Dr. Ethan. Can You also tell her they're taking super awesome care of me and that I'll see her real soon? Oh, and if there's a puppy out there who needs a home, can You bring him to me so I can love him? And... I think that's it. Amen."

Ethan was done in by a seven-year-old's sweet, heartfelt prayers.

"Now it's your turn," Flicka said.

Keely's soft voice said, "Dear Lord, thank you for bringing Felicity into my life."

His eyes squeezed tightly shut, Ethan listened to the rest of her prayer with his stomach tying into knots inside knots.

She included requests for her family and friends, mentioned the poor, the hungry and the hurting. Then he heard his name. "I pray You guide Ethan's hands as he treats his patients. And let him know he's cared for—"

"And loved," Flicka added.

"And loved," Keely said after a brief pause.

"Your turn, Dr. Ethan."

"I...don't..." He heaved a sigh. The pain in his throat made his voice deeper than usual.

"It's okay," Flicka whispered, nudging him with her shoulder. "There's no right or wrong way to pray."

"Lord," he rattled out, "I pray You keep Flicka

and Keely safe, always. And take care of the rest of my family. In, uh… Your Son's name, Amen."

He opened his eyes and caught Keely watching him with soft eyes. In that moment there was no shadow covering his soul, no pain, no sense of terrible grief. There was just Keely and this moment of incredible peace.

Flicka shifted beside him, then jumped to her feet, sufficiently breaking the mood.

"Night, Dr. Ethan." She kissed him on the cheek.

He swallowed past the golf-ball-sized lump in his throat. "Night, kiddo, sleep tight."

Eyes sparkling with little-girl satisfaction, she repeated the process with Keely.

The moment she headed upstairs to brush her teeth, Ethan stood. "I have an early morning. So I should probably—"

"You don't have to explain anything to me." She took his hand and led him to the back door. "Good night, Ethan."

Still holding on to him, she pressed a tender kiss to his cheek. The longing for something more was so powerful it stole his breath.

He stepped back and put physical distance between them. "I found the camels we need for the parade."

Her reaction was priceless, a mixture of utter shock and skepticism. "You're really through fighting me on this?"

"A smart soldier knows when to remain in battle

and when to retreat." Though he hadn't meant to speak in subtext, his words had a double meaning. By the sad look in her eyes, Keely caught both of them.

He'd hurt her again. It seemed inevitable whenever they got too close, whenever things between them seemed to take a step toward something real and lasting.

Not sure how to breach the awkwardness, not even sure he should try, he said good-night and then strode across their snow-covered backyards. He swerved around the snowman still wearing the ridiculous Christmas scarf and cowboy hat, the memory of the snowball fight clear in his mind.

The evening had been a turning point in his relationship with Keely, a glimpse of what his life could be like with her and Flicka in it.

He could see it now, the three of them sitting around a Christmas tree, a couple of dogs running wild, another child on the way...

He immediately pushed the image out of his mind.

What was the point of reaching for that kind of happiness when it could be lost at any moment?

Chapter Sixteen

With his mind in chaos, Ethan entered his house through the back door. He immediately dealt with the dogs. The brisk walk did nothing to calm his racing thoughts.

He'd enjoyed his time with Keely and Felicity. Whenever he was with them he felt at peace, finally whole again, a sensation that had been missing in his life since losing Tracy.

Tracy. He tried to draw up her image. But it was Keely's face he saw, Keely's long red hair and sea-green eyes. His beautiful neighbor challenged him with her wit, engaged his mind with her intelligence and sparked his humor with her snarky comments.

Guilt reared and he accepted the truth at last. He was falling for Keely O'Toole. He might already be in love with her.

His breath turned cold in his chest, a sensation that had nothing to do with the frigid night air. If he let himself love her, and then lost her, he'd never survive. But if he never loved her, would he really be living? He couldn't help thinking the life the Lord had planned for him included Keely.

"Let's go home, boys."

He retraced his steps, the dogs trotting happily beside him, blissfully ignorant of Ethan's inner turmoil. As he directed the animals back inside the house, he caught sight of his face in the hallway mirror. His eyes looked hollow. They matched how he felt inside. He trudged into the kitchen, filled the dog's water bowls with hands that were no longer steady.

Returning to the living room, he sank onto the couch. Too exhausted to do anything but watch television, he reached for the remote. The photo album on the coffee table caught his eye. He'd left it open to a picture of him and Tracy. Samantha had taken the shot. It was off-center and slightly blurry and that much more charming for the imperfections.

His hand hovered over the page. An ache spread through his chest. He turned the page, studied the assortment of photos. They were mostly of Tracy and Samantha, but Baloo had worked his way into several of the images.

Memory after memory slammed into him. He let them come, let them take him back in time, to another place, another life. He turned the page.

Somewhere halfway through the album, the process became less painful, more cathartic.

You want to honor Tracy's memory, start living again.

He paused at the picture of him and Samantha at the father/daughter dance. He wouldn't regret taking her, wouldn't regret filling in for her real father, if only temporarily.

Head down, he finished looking through the album. He flipped to the final page, paused. It was the same candid shot of him and Tracy in Afghanistan he kept on his desk at work.

Beside the photo was Tracy's favorite Bible verse. "And we know that all things work together for good to those who love God, to those who are the called according to His purpose."

Ethan's eyes burned over the perfectly timed message. It felt as if Tracy was giving him permission to move on.

"I love you," he whispered to the image. "You will always be in my heart, but it's time I said goodbye."

The never-ending sorrow that had lived inside him for well over a year released its tight grip. *Thank You, Lord.*

It wasn't an elegant prayer, but it was full of sincerity, the first step on his journey back to retrieving his faith, to taking back his life.

He leaned his head back, closed his eyes and let the peace that transcended all understanding fill him. At some point he must have fallen asleep, the album still on his lap.

The sound of his cell phone ringing startled him awake. He recognized the hospital's number. Setting aside the album, he answered on the fourth ring, "Dr. Scott."

"Ethan, it's me, Ryder."

The concern in his brother's voice had him snapping awake. He rubbed a hand over his face. "What's wrong?"

"Alma Collier was brought in by ambulance. She's had a heart attack."

The last of his grogginess vanished. He'd just seen the elderly woman on Saturday and had feared this moment was coming. "I'll be there shortly."

Ending the call, he checked the time, discovered it was just shy of 6:00 a.m. He showered, took care of the dogs, then, seeing lights on at Keely's house, sent her a text.

Heading to hospital. Emergency. May not be able to run home before work. Can you check on dogs later this morning?

Her response came immediately. Absolutely.

He texted his thanks.

A long pause followed, making Ethan think she wouldn't respond. He was already in his SUV, shoving his key in the ignition when her next text came through.

No words, just symbols. xoxoxo

Hugs and kisses. Despite the seriousness of the situation, and his concern for Mrs. Collier, Ethan drove away from his house feeling less alone than he had in a year and a half.

Ethan's text hadn't given Keely much information concerning the emergency that had called him away. Halfway between their yards, she lifted up a prayer for both doctor and patient.

As she stepped onto the back stoop, she couldn't help noticing the lack of Christmas decorations. No sparkling lights, no garlands, not even tacky lawn ornaments scattered in the front yard.

The Scott house looked sad, as sad as Ethan when his gaze went distant and he erected an invisible wall around himself.

What's your story, Ethan? What aren't you telling me?

Using the key he'd given her, Keely entered the house through the back. Two happy dogs greeted her. "Hello, boys."

She gave each head a pat, then pulled both animals into a group hug. Ethan's text hadn't mentioned if he'd fed them this morning. "I'm thinking a small bowl of kibble can't hurt."

She got no argument from the dogs.

As she entered the kitchen pantry, she moved with the ease of someone familiar with every corner of this house. Of course she was familiar. She'd spent considerable time here as a child. Even at the worst of her teenage years, when she'd been wrongfully labeled a terrible flirt by jealous peers, Olivia had stood by her.

Smiling, she set the bowls on the ground in front of the dogs. Baloo, polite and well trained, calmly went about eating his snack. Cupcake, on the other hand, needed a few lessons in manners. The puppy proceeded to inhale his food.

To the sound of canine crunching, Keely glanced around the kitchen. There didn't seem to be many signs of use. Such a pity. Especially since someone had gone to the trouble of updating the appliances, flooring and decorative tile.

Running her fingertips along the granite countertops, she itched to dirty things up a bit. Kitchens were meant to be used. Keely could do a lot of creating here. She could see herself feeding an entire family of kids, Ethan coming up behind her for an impromptu waltz and—

She cut off the rest of that thought and picked up the now empty bowls. Then she took the dogs outside. When they'd finished their business, she ushered them back into the house. Cupcake initiated a game of tug-of-war with Baloo and an ancient sock.

While the older dog indulged the puppy, Keely expanded her tour beyond the kitchen. The moment she stepped into the living room, she realized Ethan had forgotten to turn off the lights. Or perhaps Ryder was home from the hospital.

Doubtful. The house had an empty feel. Nevertheless, she called out, "Ryder?"

No answer.

She strolled fully into the room, glanced around at the masculine decor. The brown leather furniture and bold, solid-colored rugs were of excellent quality but lacked imagination. "Anybody home?"

Still no answer.

Keely couldn't help herself. She worked her way through the room, shutting off lights as she went.

As she was nearly finished with the task, her gaze fell on the coffee table, zeroing in on what looked like a scrapbook, or maybe a photo album. Keely sat on the sofa and studied the book without actually picking it up.

The various pictures depicted a happy family caught in candid poses. The father had dark hair cut military short. The mother had long golden blond hair. The young daughter was full of smiles. There was even a family dog, a black Lab, about the same age as Baloo, and—

What, exactly, had she stumbled upon? Whose family was this?

Maybe the album belonged to Ethan's youngest brother, Brody. It was certainly possible. Brody was in some foreign country working for Doctors Without Borders. He could easily have left something this personal behind for safekeeping.

As she leaned forward for a better look, a sob rose in her throat. That wasn't Brody in the pictures. It was Ethan.

She yanked up the album, focused on one of the images. Ethan's arm was slung over the beautiful woman's shoulders. She was smiling up at him. The love in their eyes was evident. The little girl, a miniature version of the woman, had her hand on Baloo's back.

Caught up in the joy that leaped off the pages, Keely continued flipping through the album. It didn't take her long to realize this was no casual relationship. Had Ethan been married?

There were no wedding pictures. And yet the people in the photographs were the very essence of family.

Hands shaking now, Keely turned to the back page, to a picture of Ethan and the woman in matching battle fatigues. Unable to stop herself, she started back at the beginning, this time stopping on several images of the woman in a flight suit, posing in and out of a helicopter.

Despair filled Keely. She thought she and Ethan were growing close, maybe even building the kind of connection that would last a lifetime. She'd been wrong, so wrong. Here, in her hands, was evidence that she knew very little about her neighbor, and nothing of the man in this album.

"What happened to you?" she whispered to the woman smiling up at her. Something tragic;

nothing else explained the sadness she often sensed in Ethan.

Keely had fallen for a man she hardly knew, a man who still held on to a woman from his past.

Feeling like an interloper, she set aside the book and closed her eyes. She'd been in this place before, in love with a man who still clung to the woman no longer in his life. She knew how this ended. In heartache. *Her* heartache.

It was exactly the wake-up call she needed.

After leaving the hospital, with Mrs. Collier in critical but stable condition, the rest of Ethan's morning remained busy. On his lunch break, he made his usual trip home to let the dogs out.

As soon as he entered the house, he knew Keely had followed through with her promise to check on them this morning. All the lights were out, something neither he nor Ryder ever remembered to do. As the dogs danced around him in a tail-wagging frenzy, the fine hairs on the back of his neck prickled.

Something felt...off.

Unable to pinpoint what, he moved into the living room and froze. The photo album wasn't where he left it.

Had Keely moved it, or Ryder?

The easiest way to find out would be to wake up his brother. Yeah, like that would go over well.

Leaving Ryder to his sleep, Ethan took care of

the dogs, then drove back to town, determined to get answers, even if they weren't the ones he wanted. It would be tempting to return to his office, ignore the nagging sensation in his gut, pretend the pulse beating in his ears meant nothing.

Ethan was through taking the easy way out. No more putting off the inevitable. He made the trip from parking lot to Keely's restaurant with ground-eating strides. The moment he pushed into Senor O'Toole's, a wall of heat and noise hit him.

The restaurant was full of holiday shoppers. There wasn't a free table in the place, but the stool at the counter where he usually ate remained free. Weaving his way through the crowd, he claimed his regular position. Keely had her back to him as she manned the soda machine, filling drink glasses with the speed and efficiency he'd grown to expect of her.

As if sensing his eyes on her, she glanced over her shoulder. The shaky smile she gave him was a haunting echo of the wariness he himself felt. The way she held her shoulders, at a cautious angle told him all he needed to know.

She'd seen the photo album.

Ethan's gut rolled, his heart filled with remorse. He should have told Keely about Tracy long before now.

Keely's smile remained stiff around the edges, her eyes filled with what almost looked like pain.

Yeah, he should have told her about Tracy.

Drawing in a bracing breath, he got straight to the point. "We need to talk."

She flinched at his abrupt tone. But after only a brief hesitation, she motioned for one of her waiters to take over at the soda machine and approached Ethan.

With the counter a physical barrier between, they stared at each other for a long moment, neither speaking, neither moving. Then, as if coming to a hard decision, Keely reached out and closed her hand over his.

Ethan wanted to whisk her away, to protect her from the pain he saw in her eyes, the pain he'd unwittingly inflicted on her. "Keely, I realize you saw the—"

She stopped him midspeech with a gentle squeeze to his hand. With her hand still linked with his, she said, "I owe you an apology."

She was apologizing to *him*?

"When I was in your house this morning, I noticed you'd left all the lights on in the living room. Long story short, I saw the photo album you left on the coffee table and looked through it. I'm sorry, Ethan."

"There's nothing to be sorry for."

Breaking eye contact, she pulled her hand away, worked the edges of a bar towel between her fingers. "I didn't mean to intrude on your privacy. There's simply no excuse."

"I should have told you about—"

"Keely!" a masculine voice bellowed from the kitchen, sufficiently cutting off the rest of Ethan's speech. "Get in here, quick."

She gave him an apologetic grimace. "I'll be right back."

When she returned, she had a difficult time meeting his gaze. Their conversation was clearly making her uncomfortable. Ethan pressed on anyway. "I should have told you about Tracy."

"Tracy." She spoke the name so softly he wasn't sure she'd actually said it out loud. "Is that the woman in the photos?"

"Yes."

The muscles in her jaw bunched and her fingers shook as she continued to pick at the towel in her hand.

"I want to tell you about her. But you're busy. And I have to get back to the office soon. I'll come over later this evening, after Flicka goes to bed, and we'll talk then."

"It'll be late. Tonight is the father/daughter dance at the church."

The dance. He'd forgotten all about it. "Text me when she falls asleep."

"Okay." She opened her mouth to say something else, but was once again called into the kitchen.

As Ethan watched her make her way through the swinging doors, he desperately wanted to tell her they'd work things out and maybe even find a way to be together. Not as friends or neighbors, but as a couple.

Was he willing to set aside his fear of losing her? He wanted to try. With love came loss, but without love life was nothing more than existing. He was tired of just existing. He wanted more and wanted it with Keely.

But he wasn't free of the past just yet. There was a ragged loose end that needed tying up first.

Having lost his appetite, he returned to the medical clinic without eating lunch. He waved off questions, stepped into his private office and shut the door firmly behind him.

Working on his laptop, he searched for the proper website and booked a flight from Denver to South Carolina for Friday afternoon, with a return flight two days later. The cost was ridiculous and he'd be gone just over forty-eight hours. But when Ethan pulled into his driveway Sunday evening, the night before Christmas Eve, he would be free to begin the rest of his life.

Would Keely be a part of it?

For the first time in a year and a half, he wanted to take a leap of faith. It would take courage and prayer to commit to another woman. He lifted up a petition to the Lord, for guidance, clear direction and the courage to step out into the unknown future.

After his last patient was gone, he returned to

his office, pulled out his phone and made the call he'd put off long enough.

Phyllis Jenkins answered on the first ring. "Ethan, I'm so happy to hear from you."

"I'm coming to the memorial," he said without preamble.

"Oh, that's…" A sob sounded in his ear. "…so very…" Another sob. "…wonderful."

"Thanks for inviting me."

"It wouldn't feel right without you."

They talked for another fifteen minutes. He disconnected the call to the tune of female tears of gratitude. Setting the phone on his desk, he continued to stare at the blank screen.

A scratching on his doorjamb had him looking up and staring into a pale, taut face, the very embodiment of physical pain.

Ethan quickly rounded his desk. "Sit down, Beau, before you fall over."

The stubborn man remained propped against the doorframe, practically turned inside himself, cradling his elbow in his palm. Ethan took the bulk of his weight and guided him to a chair. "Let me guess, you went skiing this afternoon."

"If you're going to say I told you so," Beau gritted out, "I suggest you pause and reflect."

Not intimidated in the least, Ethan gave his friend a long look. "You gonna tell me what happened?"

"I went skiing this afternoon. I took a turn

too tight and had to overcorrect and might have tweaked my injury a bit."

"Tweaked your injury," Ethan repeated, amazed at the guy's gift for understatement.

"Look, Ethan." Beau blew out a hard, frustrated hiss of air. "I'm on a time crunch here. Give me a shot of cortisone or whatever it takes to help me manage the pain long enough to dress for the dance and we're good."

The dance. Right, that was tonight. "What time are you supposed to pick up Flicka?"

"Just before seven." He ground out the words through clenched teeth, gasping for air as Ethan helped him stand and then steered him down the hallway.

Clearly, the guy was in a lot of pain. That he came into the office spoke volumes.

"Well?" Beau gave him a hopeful look reminiscent of Baloo begging for a dog treat. "You gonna hook me up with something to help me get dressed without collapsing?"

"No can do. I'm not that kind of doctor."

Beau frowned. "I thought you were my friend."

"I am. Which is why we're doing this right, starting with X-rays."

He set the world champ of pigheadedness in exam room 1 and then tracked down Tasha.

"We have a last-minute patient."

"Let's get to it, then. I have date in an hour."

One look at the X-rays told Ethan that Beau

wasn't going to make the dance. He gave him the bad news, plus a prescription for pain medication.

"No pills," Beau ground out.

Proving he meant business, he tore the prescription into shreds. Even that simple task took effort, if the sweat pouring down his face was any indication.

"But you're in pain."

"I'll gut it out."

Ethan shook his head. "What about tonight?" he asked. "You gonna gut out the entire dance?"

"The dance isn't the concern. Dressing for the event…" He sighed heavily. "That could be a problem."

The guy wasn't only stubborn he was delusional. "I'll cover for you tonight."

"Wow, Doc, aren't you the stand-up guy?" Beau's tone was full of irony, but did nothing to deter Ethan now that the idea was in his head.

Later, as he stood in his bedroom, working the black tie hanging around his neck into a respectable bow, he thought of Tracy, of her favorite Bible verse scrolled on the pages of the photo album. "And we know that all things work together for good to those who love God, to those who are the called according to His purpose."

It was as if God had been leading Ethan to this moment all his life. Every heartache, every tragedy, every loss had brought him to this place, at this time. Tracy would always be in his heart, but he couldn't keep living in the past. As a pastor once told him, and Connor reiterated, clinging to the dead was no way to live.

The future was within his grasp. All he had to do was reach for it. Did he have the courage?

Chapter Seventeen

Keely's cell phone dinged with an incoming text, but as her hands were busy wrestling Felicity's hair into a complicated updo she could only glance at the screen. It was from her brother.

As she twisted, twirled and bent locks of the little girl's hair, she lifted up a silent prayer that whatever Beau had texted wasn't bad news.

She ignored the phone a bit longer. She'd had quite enough troubling news for one day, starting with the photo album she'd stumbled upon this morning and Ethan's promise to discuss Tracy with Keely later tonight.

A wave of intense jealousy tried to take hold. Keely refused to give in to the emotion. So Ethan had a past. Well, Keely did, too. Not many people made it into their late twenties without some kind of romantic history trailing after them.

She cared for Ethan, maybe even loved him. Nothing he said would change that. Unfortunately, what he said could affect their future and whether there was a chance for them to be together.

Her phone buzzed again, obnoxiously reminding her she hadn't opened the text from her brother.

"You want me to get your phone for you?" Felicity asked from her position in front of the mirror. "I can reach it if I stretch out my arm real far."

"No need. I'm just about finished." Keely tucked the last strand of hair beneath the crystal tiara, bobby-pinned it in place, then nodded in satisfaction. "It's official. I've still got the touch."

"Can I see?"

"Absolutely." She handed Felicity a small mirror, turned her around, then showed her how to position the glass so she could view the back of her head.

"I love it! It's the best hairstyle ever!"

Keely bit back a laugh. Apparently, Baloo was the best dog ever. Out in the backyard stood the best snowman ever. They'd picked out the best Christmas tree ever, and so on.

Well, as far as Keely was concerned, Felicity was the best kid ever. She pressed a kiss to the child's cheek. "Time to get into your dress."

"Yay." She skipped and twirled out of the room.

Now that she was alone, Keely picked up her phone and frowned at the message from her brother. Change of plans. Ethan filling in for me tonight. He'll pick up the kid at your place.

Worry for her brother had her typing out a quick text, asking him if he was okay.

I'm fine.

The cryptic response only added to her worry. Thumbs flying across the screen, she asked if he needed her to come over.

His curt, one-word answer—don't—ended the conversation, but not Keely's determination to find out what had happened to her brother. Seeking answers, she texted Ethan next.

His response was nearly as curt as her brother's. She huffed out a breath. "Doctor-patient confidentiality, indeed."

Beau had obviously blown out his shoulder again.

Keely was half tempted to call her mother and tattle on him, but her brother was a grown man.

Sighing, Keely debated whether to tell the little girl about the change in plans, then decided to let her be surprised when Ethan arrived on their doorstep.

"Felicity?" she called out. "Need help getting dressed?"

"Nope. All done." Felicity's door swung open and out she twirled, her red-and-green Christmas dress sparkling in the overhead lights.

She spun again, and again and again, then finally stopped. "So? How do I look?"

"Oh, Felicity." Keely sniffled back a wave of emotion that felt suspiciously like maternal pride.

"You look absolutely beautiful. Like a fairy-tale princess come to life."

"I feel like a princess. Thank you." She threw herself at Keely. "Thank you for being my mom while mine is gone. I love you so much."

"I love you, too, baby, with all my heart." The doorbell kept her from blubbering all over the child.

Keely let Felicity open the door.

The little girl's squeal of delight matched her own reaction to the man standing on their front stoop, holding a wrist corsage of tiny red roses in a clear plastic box.

Okay, it was true, nearly every man on the planet looked good in a tuxedo. But Ethan, with his black hair, masculine features and startling blue eyes, took the sophisticated suit to a whole new level.

"Is that for me?" Felicity asked, pointing to the corsage.

"It is." He stepped inside the house, shut the door behind him and gave all his attention to the little girl.

Felicity twirled.

"Wow, Flicka. You look like a princess."

She twirled again. "Keely just said the very same thing."

Eyebrows raised, he glanced at Keely over the child's head. There was something in his expression, something besides warmth, a silent promise her heart understood but her mind couldn't quite grasp.

The look in his eyes said that Ethan cared for her in a way that went beyond friendship. Was it possible his feelings for her were as strong as hers for him?

She nearly wobbled, forced her knees to lock. "I'll get your coat, Felicity."

When she returned, Ethan was telling Felicity he hoped they played the chicken dance song at least once.

"What's the chicken dance?"

"I won't spoil it for you, but let's just say you're in for a treat." As he helped the child into her coat, he smiled over at Keely. "What time's our curfew, Mom?"

Her heart dipped to her toes. Could this man be any more charming? Playing along, she gave a stern wag of her finger. "Ten o'clock, sharp. Not a minute after or you'll answer to me."

They all laughed.

Before leading the little girl outside, Ethan pulled Keely into his arms for a brief hug. "I'll see you later tonight."

"I'll be here waiting."

"Good, we have a lot to talk about, you and me."

Oh, boy, did they ever!

At precisely three minutes shy of 10:00 p.m., Ethan guided Flicka up Keely's front walk. Ever since climbing into his SUV in the church parking lot, the kid had been a nonstop chatterbox, going on and on about the fun she'd had at the dance. "Did you have fun, Dr. Ethan?"

He slung his arm over her shoulder. "I did."

Far more than he'd expected.

There'd been a moment, right after they first entered the all-purpose room at the church, when memories of another father/daughter dance had hit him. But then Flicka had caught sight of the area where formal pictures were being taken. Unaware of his turmoil, she'd grabbed his hand and begged to get a photograph with him.

The joy in her face had pulled him back into the moment, where he'd stayed the rest of the evening. The men's ministry had gone all out. There'd been games, line dances with helpful instructions from the older girls, an excellent dinner and, to top off the evening, the infamous chicken dance.

"What was your favorite part of the night?" he asked.

"Oh, that's easy. The chicken dance."

That had been his favorite part, too.

Without knocking, the kid burst through the front door and sped into the living room as if she lived there, which, of course, she did. But the ease and familiarity of the move weren't lost on Ethan. Every day the child was becoming more comfortable in her new home. There was, indeed, hope for the future.

"Keely! Keely, where are you?"

The woman in question entered the room, her gaze landing on the child's face. "Well? Did you have a good time tonight?"

"It was the best dance ever!"

A secretive smile spread across Keely's features. "Somehow I knew you were going to say that."

Flicka laughed.

"Hey, Keely, look what I can do now." An enthusiastic rendition of the chicken dance, tune included, followed the command.

Keely dutifully watched and clapped along and even hummed several bars of the song. The affection in her eyes was unmistakable, as were the tears she valiantly fought off with several fast blinks.

It was a full ten minutes before the kid wound down. By then Ethan thought his heart might explode with love for the woman and child who had come into his life one cold Sunday evening nearly a month ago. He didn't want to lose them.

"Dr. Ethan and I got you this." Flicka dug into the goody bag she'd received at the end of the night. She rooted around a bit, then produced the photograph they'd taken upon first arriving at the church.

"It's…oh, it's lovely."

While Keely battled another bout of tears, the excitement of the evening finally caught up with

Flicka. Her loud, jaw-cracking yawn was followed by a second one, and then a third.

Smiling softly, Keely brushed a hand over the little girl's cheek. "Time for bed, sleepyhead."

"I am pretty tired." With one last surge of energy, she launched herself at Ethan, gave him a fierce hug. "Thanks for being my daddy tonight."

"You're welcome." His voice came out low and gruff. He wanted desperately to make promises that he would be her daddy for years to come, but something held him back. A mix of loyalty to his former life and a need to find closure before making promises.

"I'll never forget the fun we had tonight."

"Neither will I." He kissed the top of her head, then set her away from him. "Sleep tight, sweetheart."

"Okay."

Thanking him with her eyes, Keely ushered the child toward the stairs and told Ethan to make himself comfortable.

True to her word, she returned fifteen minutes later. By the time she joined him on the couch, Ethan had shed his coat and suit jacket, pulled loose his tie and propped up his feet on a nearby ottoman.

"She's already asleep. Oh, Ethan, I think she's finally settling into her new life."

"That would be my diagnosis."

She laughed. The relief in the sound was unmistakable and Ethan felt the last of the ice around his heart melt away. He patted the empty spot beside him. "Come sit down and we'll have that talk I promised."

Her gaze wary now, instead of settling in beside him, she chose the chair on the other side of the coffee table. The lights of the Christmas tree sparkled behind her, adding a soft, homey feel to the room, and to the moment, bringing the surety of what Ethan wanted, what he craved.

"Will you tell me, that is…" Her gaze darted around the room. "Will you tell me about Tracy now?"

"Yes." He lowered his feet to the floor, leaned his elbows on his knees and held her stare. "But now that the time is here, I'm not sure where to start."

Keely's face turned soft, kind. "Who was she to you? Your girlfriend?"

"My fiancée."

The revelation didn't seem to surprise her. But her shoulders bunched and she crossed her arms around her waist. "The little girl in the pictures. She was Tracy's daughter?"

He nodded, and then, in a voice without inflection, he told the story of the woman he'd lost. "I met Tracy in Afghanistan. It was love at first sight for us both, but we didn't date until we were stateside."

Now that he'd begun, the words spilled from his

mouth. He told Keely things he'd never told anyone, not even his siblings. With each revelation, he could feel the past releasing its grip.

"I proposed six months after our first date. I was completely committed to becoming a husband to her and a father to her daughter, Samantha."

He detailed his and Tracy's plans to stay in the army. Then, with his mind poised between past and present, no longer able to sit, he took to pacing the perimeter of the room.

Keely held silent, watching him closely yet giving him the time he needed to gather his thoughts.

In a halting voice, he told her about the car accident that had taken Tracy's life, about the terrible call that had been eerily similar to the one he'd received the night of his parents' crash. All the grief and agony he'd once felt reared up, threatening to tug him under.

At some point, Keely had jumped to her feet and crossed the room to where he now stood frozen in memories. She drew him into her arms and held on, saying nothing, simply allowing him to calm his breathing.

"I'm sorry for your loss," she whispered, her cheek pressed against his bent head.

For several seconds he simply stood in the circle of Keely's comforting embrace, allowing her kindness, her understanding—her very presence—to erase another layer of the pain he'd buried deep within his heart. The final step toward healing, toward letting go of his past, still eluded him.

"Tracy's mother called me." Stepping back, he explained about the memorial service and what Phyllis requested of him.

"Are you going to scatter her ashes?"

"I need the closure."

He admitted that now, as he stared into Keely's eyes, wanting to take a chance on her, on them, but not yet fully free to do so. "I fly out Friday afternoon and, barring any delays, will be home Sunday night. I'll miss the last parade meeting, but not the parade itself."

"I understand."

He took her face in his hands. It wasn't solely her outward beauty that called to him, that made him want to wake up, to live again, to risk another loss for the sake of love. It was Keely herself, her sly wit and the warm heart that lurked beneath her snarky exterior.

"Do you understand why I'm telling you about Tracy?"

Eyes unspeakably sad, she nodded very slowly, very carefully. "You want me to know how much you still love her."

"Of course I still love her. I'll always love her. She's a part of me." He held her gaze, wanting her to hear the truth from him, only him. "I'm the man I am because of knowing her."

With each word he spoke, he felt the last of his

grief lifting, the past finally releasing him. But instead of joy filling Keely's eyes, instead of understanding and relief, she looked defeated, devastated even, as if he'd taken a scalpel to her heart and was carving away. "I've hurt you."

She nodded, tears filling her eyes.

"I'm sorry." He didn't know what else to say, so he addressed the issue head-on. "Tell me how I can fix it."

Chapter Eighteen

Keely's heart was breaking, shattering at her feet, because of the man standing before her. And just like every other time in their tumultuous past, Ethan had no idea of the impact his words were having on her. But this time, she would tell him. No more evasion, no more jumping to conclusions.

His words echoed in her mind, torturing her. *I still love her. I'll always love her. She's a part of me.*

Keely forced back a sob. She'd heard a variation of those words once before, the day Cutter had taken back his proposal.

Ethan might as well have stuck a dagger in her heart. In that moment, Keely knew she loved him, but he would never be hers, not completely. The tears she'd ruthlessly held at bay demanded release. She gave up the fight and let them come.

She spun around, presenting her back to the man she loved. Not for one more second could she look into Ethan's intense blue eyes, eyes shadowed with memories from his past.

"Keely." He came up behind her, drew her back against his broad chest. "Talk to me."

For one, blissful second she allowed his strength to swallow her grief.

She would have given him her heart, her future, her everything. They would have been good together, happy, if only his heart was free to love her in return.

His hands closed over her shoulders, and he slowly turned her around to face him. "I've hurt you. You must realize that was never my intention."

"Oh, Ethan, I know that."

He placed a knuckle beneath her chin and applied gentle pressure until her gaze once again met his. "Would you rather me not have told you about Tracy?"

"No." She said the word in a rush of air. "I'm honored you shared your past with me. I'm sorry for your loss, Ethan, so very sorry. You've suffered a great tragedy." He'd lost the love of his life in a car accident, just as he'd lost his parents. How did he bear it? How did he make it from one day to the next?

His strength humbled her.

"Tell me why you're crying. Why do I get the feeling I've just broken your heart?"

Honesty goes both ways, she reminded herself.

"You shared your past with me. It's only fair I share mine with you."

The look of utter shock on his face would have been comical under any other circumstances.

"I'm nearly thirty years old, Ethan. Did you think I made it through my twenties without a single relationship or heartbreak?"

He speared a hand through his hair. "I don't know what I thought. But when you put it that way, it makes sense you would have experienced at least one breakup."

"It was far more devastating than a simple breakup."

Hand clasped in his, she led him back to the couch, waited until they were both settled to tell him about her disastrous romance with Cutter.

When she finished the tale of how they met— at a party thrown by mutual friends—she paused to gather her words. "We were perfectly suited for each other. Our goals for the future were the same and we really got along, better than most friends and certainly better than most couples we knew."

"If you were that good together, why aren't you with him?"

"It's complicated."

"You listened to my story. Give me a chance to hear yours."

It was only fair. "I knew Cutter was getting ready to ask me to marry him. He'd even taken me ring shopping. Then, when he told me he was taking me to dinner at our favorite restaurant, and that I should dress for the occasion, I knew he was going to pop the question."

"Did he ask you to marry him that night?"

Pain slashed through her heart. "During dessert. We were happy for a time, a few weeks, but I could feel Cutter pulling away emotionally. And then..." She couldn't get the words out. They simply vanished.

Ethan took her hand. The gesture gave her the strength to continue. "And then, one day, Cutter asked for the ring back."

"Did he give you a reason?"

Sorrow and humiliation filled her. "He said he wasn't ready to get married, because he wasn't over his wife."

"He was divorced?"

"A widower. His wife died of cancer two years before we met." She slowly pulled her hand free, lifted her chin, held his stare. "When he asked for the ring back, his exact words were 'I'm not ready to marry you. I still love Pamela.'"

"Keely, listen to me." Ethan's voice took on a desperate note. "I told you about Tracy because I'm ready to let her go. I'm ready to move on. With you. I want to be with you and I think you want to be with me. Am I wrong?"

She shook her head, unable to lie about something so important.

"That's why I'm going to the memorial service,

to deal with the past, so I can move into the future. I hope to do that with you."

His sincerity was real. But would it last?

Would he go to the memorial service and realize he wasn't ready to move on?

She couldn't take that kind of blow again.

"It's late." She shifted out from under his touch. "It's been an emotional night for us both. Let's take a break, talk again tomorrow, or the day after that, or maybe next week."

Like a boulder cemented to concrete, Ethan held his ground. "We can table this discussion, if that's what you want. But I'm not going to change my mind about you, or us."

The promise was there in his eyes, yet no words of love.

"I'm tired, Ethan. Please, go home, we'll talk again soon."

"I'm *not* going to change my mind," he repeated, taming a stray wisp of hair behind her ear. The tenderness in the gesture teased hope to the surface. She ruthlessly shut it down. He himself said he needed closure.

Keely desperately wanted to believe Ethan. Cutter had been equally sincere. He, too, had meant the words he'd said, until he took them all back.

"I'm leaving for Tracy's memorial Friday afternoon. When I return, we'll talk." He pressed a light kiss to her temple, her cheek, then her lips. "Think of me while I'm gone."

How could she not?

Ethan wordlessly picked up his jacket, then his coat, then walked out the front door.

The soft click of metal meeting metal told Keely she was alone. Very alone. More alone than she'd ever felt in her entire life.

Keely didn't think about Ethan for the next three days. She didn't think about him when she gave the all clear signal to Ryder so he could let the dogs into the backyard.

She didn't think about him at the final parade meeting where she and the committee addressed last minute details. She didn't think about him when she and Felicity built another snowman, or when they made snow ice cream or...

Who was she kidding? she asked herself, as she prepared dinner for her and Felicity. Keely did nothing *but* think about Ethan. And every time she did, she prayed for him. *Lord, give him the closure he's seeking.*

He would be home late this evening. Would he call her? He said he would, but what if he didn't? Sighing, she looked out the window, noted that snow was coming down heavier than forecasted.

"Keely?" Felicity hovered in the doorway, her face pinched in pain. "I don't feel so good."

She forced her legs to move quickly, then crouched in front of the child. "Is it your tummy?"

Hand pressed over her mouth, she nodded. "Will you call Dr. Ethan and ask him to come over?"

"I can't, baby. He's still out of town."

The child's big blue eyes flickered with despair. "But...but...I really miss him. Can't you make him come home?"

If only it were that simple.

"He is coming home, but not for several hours yet." If the storm worsened and they closed the airports, he might not make it home until tomorrow, or the day after that. Information Keely did not share with her little cousin.

"Let's get you in the bed until you feel better."

They barely made it three steps before Felicity's face went dead white and she lost the contents of her stomach on Keely's shoes. Her first instinct was to call Ethan, but he wasn't home. And Ryder was working the night shift at the hospital.

Helplessness danced a chill up her spine. She had two choices, stand here wringing her hands, or take Felicity to the ER. Keely knew what she had to do. As she helped the child in her car, then backed out of the drive, she could hear nothing but the sound of her pulse drumming in her ears.

Keely took the quickest route to the hospital, around town, instead of through it, where there would be no stoplights or ridiculously slow speed limits.

Snow came down hard, making visibility nearly impossible. She didn't see the black ice, had no way to correct her course by time she did. The steering wheel jerked out of her hands. The Jeep went into a fast skid, too fast. She steered into the turn, but couldn't regain control.

As her car slipped toward an embankment, Keely's first thought was of the child in the backseat. She prayed Felicity wouldn't be hurt. *Please, Lord, keep her safe.*

Her next thought was of Ethan, and what this accident would do to him. And then…

Everything went black.

On the drive home from Denver International Airport, Ethan concentrated on the road. The snow was coming down hard, but he wanted to get home, needed to get home. To Keely, the woman he loved. As he thought back over their relationship, he recognized that the two of them had been building to this moment for nearly a year.

In the silence of his SUV, he practiced his speech, reviewing what he would say to convince Keely he was ready to commit his future to hers.

He got the call from Ryder a mile out of town. His brother's voice came to him as if from a long, dark tunnel. His mind latched on to two words. *Car accident.*

Then two more. *Keely* and *Felicity.*

His heart turned cold as ice and empty as the night. He couldn't lose Keely and Flicka. He thought of all the time he'd wasted, holding them both at a distance, when he could have enjoyed them more, loved them more, given them his entire heart.

The spiral of regret and fear threatened to pull him under. He pulled his own SUV to a stop and asked, "How badly are they hurt?"

"They're fine, Ethan. Mostly bumps and bruises, but I thought you would want to know about the accident."

"You were right. Tell Keely I'll be there in ten minutes."

"I thought you were out of town."

"Just got home." No, he wasn't home, not yet. Not until Keely was with him, and Flicka. Only then would he be home.

He disconnected the call and pulled back onto the highway.

The ten minutes it took to make the journey from the edge of town felt like an eternity. Patience ready to snap, he burst into the ER, found Ryder, who took him to where Keely was filling out paperwork and Flicka was nowhere in sight.

Was she all right?

Anticipating his question, Ryder told him, "Felicity's fine. One of the nurses took her to get Jell-O in the cafeteria."

His brother's explanation poured warmth over his cold fear. Relief nearly buckled his knees. He made his way toward Keely, ran his gaze from her head to her toes, saw nothing but the bumps and bruises Ryder promised.

"Keely."

"Ethan." She cast aside the clipboard and rushed into his arms.

He held on to her for a long, wordless moment. With her wrapped in the circle of his arms, and his hand stroking over her silky hair, he felt a moment of incredible peace. Spending the rest of his life without her by his side was no longer an option. "Don't ever scare me like that again."

"Oh, Ethan, I scared myself." She sobbed into his shirt. "What if I'd killed Felicity?"

"You didn't." The idea was too terrible to contemplate.

"She was feeling sick and I didn't know what to do. So I bundled her up and drove her to the hospital. But there was a patch of black ice on the road and…and…" She trailed off, clutched at his shirt. "I lost control of the Jeep."

A sudden image of a similar crash insinuated itself in his mind. He ruthlessly shoved it aside. "What matters is you're both okay."

He said the words as much for himself as for her.

"I'm so sorry."

"I am, too." He lowered his head, pressed his lips to hers. It was more than a kiss he gave her, but also a promise.

When he pulled away, she blinked up at him with her heart in her eyes. He saw the love shining in their depths, and the fear, the hope, all the same emotions swirling inside him.

"I don't want to go another day, wishing I had said this one moment sooner. I love you, Keely O'Toole."

"I love you, too, Ethan."

Wanting privacy for what he had to say, he drew Keely into an alcove off the waiting room, pressed another kiss to her lips. "When I came home to Village Green, I was convinced I would never love again. In my life, love came with loss and I didn't want to ever experience grief again like I did when Tracy died."

The pain that flashed in Keely's eyes had him wanting to sugarcoat the rest of his speech. That wouldn't be fair to either of them.

"My heart was locked in the past with Tracy. But then you showed up. You, Keely, with your wit and humor and snarky personality, and despite our shaky beginning, I've come to believe God Himself had a hand in drawing us together."

"And yet you avoided me for nearly a year."

He winced at the accuracy of her claim. "I avoided you because you made me uneasy, made me want to grasp for something I'd lost, to build new dreams in the place of old."

Bare your heart, Ethan. Give her your truth.

"I will always love Tracy. I won't dishonor her memory and say otherwise. But I'm not looking to replace her." He knuckled an errant curl out of her eyes. "I want to start something new, with you. What we build together will be different than what I had with Tracy, yet just as wonderful, just as genuine and lasting."

"I want that, too. But I come as a package deal."

"Flicka's a great kid and I want to help you raise her, no matter how long she's in our care."

Eyes shining, she smiled. "I'm pretty sure that can be arranged."

There was so much more he wanted to say, so much he wanted to tell her, to proclaim and promise. But he didn't want to bear his heart in a hospital waiting room. And they had a little girl probably wondering where they were.

"Then let's find Flicka and go home."

"I like the way you think, Dr. Scott."

Ethan showed up for breakfast at Keely's the morning of the parade, at precisely 6:00 a.m. Keely opened the back door and ushered him out of the cold.

"You have to eat fast," she said. "We're due downtown in thirty minutes."

"Good morning to you, too." Humor tinged his words, while intent wavered in his eyes. A second later, he swooped in for a kiss.

She let herself linger in his arms. The moment he'd arrived at the hospital after her accident, every doubt in her heart had vanished. Ethan loved her. And she loved him in return. "I love you, Ethan. I —"

Felicity's voice coming from the kitchen cut her off. "Please tell me you two aren't kissing out there."

Laughing, Ethan took Keely's hand and dragged her with him into the kitchen. "Maybe we were, and maybe we weren't."

The little girl made a gagging sound, but it was clear by the happiness in her eyes that she was pleased they were together.

The next two hours went by in a blur.

After eating a quick breakfast of yogurt and protein bars, they left the house and arrived downtown two hours prior to the start of the parade. Ethan and Keely went their separate ways.

Once she'd done all she could as the parade chair, Keely set aside her micromanaging tendencies and left the remaining details in the hands of her competent team. Walkie-talkie turned on to the proper channel, she guided Felicity to a spot on the sidewalk one block from the finish line.

They'd barely settled in when the Mitchell twins rushed over and begged Keely to let Felicity watch the parade with them. The little girl gave her a hopeful expression. "Can I?"

"Where are your parents?"

"Over there." Molly pointed across the street. Olivia and Connor waved.

Making her decision for her, the walkie-talkie

went off with a request for her immediate assistance at the Rotarian float. "Okay, you can go, but don't leave the area until I come get you after the parade."

As soon as the girls raced across the empty street, Keely climbed into her golf cart and sped back to the starting line.

Other than the minor issue of a broken part easily fixed on the Rotarian float, the parade started on time and proceeded without a hitch.

The crowd roared with laughter when the last float started down the course. Santa's sleigh being pulled by camels received the expected cheers and applause.

Ethan, otherwise known as Santa, waved to the cheering spectators while several prominent members of the community dressed as elves tossed out miniature candy canes. Keely willed him to look in her direction. The moment he noticed her, she lifted her hand, froze midwave.

That wasn't Ethan giving the crowd a jolly ho-ho-ho. It was his brother, Ryder. "Where's Ethan?" she wondered aloud.

"Right behind you."

She spun around and stared into the smiling face of the man she loved. She attempted a scowl, but couldn't quite pull it off. He looked far too handsome with that sheepish grin on his face. "Why aren't you on the float like you promised?"

"Although I do kind of like it when you scold me, Ryder volunteered to take my place."

"How much did you pay him to volunteer?"

"Aw, Keely." He placed a hand to his heart, staggered a step back. "I'm wounded you would think I'd do such a thing."

"How much?"

"Let's just say, my brother is doing me a favor that will require a large one in return."

She couldn't help it, she laughed at him. "Oh, Ethan, I love you. Don't ever change."

"Only for the better, babe."

It was a promise she would treasure for the rest of her life.

"I love you," he whispered for her ears only. "I want to grow old with you."

"I think that can be arranged."

"I'm not giving you a chance to change your mind." He took her hand, pulled her around the corner and then, once they were shielded from gawkers, dropped to one knee. "Keely O'Toole, will you marry me?"

"Yes. Yes, Ethan, I'll marry you, as soon as we can set a date."

Still holding her hand, he rose to his feet, pulled her in for a quick kiss. "God has blessed me with love twice in my life. It's more than I deserve and nothing I take for granted. I love you, Keely, with all my heart."

She believed him. "I love you, too, Ethan."

"I promise to spend the rest of my days loving you with all that I am. I will protect you and keep you safe and build a happy, fulfilling life with you."

"I'll do the same, Ethan." She rose onto her toes and kissed him on the mouth. "I will love you until the day I die."

Epilogue

Ethan's Christmas morning started an hour before the sun made its initial appearance over the horizon. By six thirty he was showered and dressed in jeans and a red sweater. He opted out of shaving. Rubbing his hand over the day-old stubble, he padded down the stairs in socks, no shoes.

It took him another ten minutes to feed the dogs.

While they gobbled up their breakfast, Ethan shoved his feet into a pair of combat boots and grabbed his coat. He let the animals out the front door, where Felicity's Christmas present joined Baloo in sniffing every bush and barren flower bed within a fifty-foot radius.

At five minutes to seven, Ethan was through waiting for the sun to rise. It was Christmas morning. He had presents to deliver and two females to spoil.

It took him considerable effort tying the shiny

red ribbon around Cupcake's neck. Apparently, the animal thought Ethan had invented a new game.

"Hold still, you furry mutt." Sometime overnight the dog had turned into a greased pig. "I mean it. Stop squirming, Cupcake."

The puppy perked up at the sound of his name and swiped his tongue across Ethan's chin.

"Enough." After a bit of unnecessary roughhousing, he finally managed to tie the ribbon into a respectable bow. "You look very pretty."

Cupcake gave him a doggy grin.

Ethan grabbed the engagement ring he'd fished out of the safe last night, then turned his attention onto the dogs. "All right, boys, let's go spend the best day of the year with our two favorite girls."

Minutes later, the puppy tucked under his arm like a football and Baloo standing politely by his side, Ethan knocked on Keely's back door. It opened with a whoosh.

"What took you so long?" The impatience in her tone was reminiscent of the last time she'd uttered the same words, the night he'd come over to check on a sick child. The night his life had changed forever, and certainly for the better.

He grinned, probably looking as dopey as the puppy in his arms. "Came as fast as I could."

As if caught up in the same memory, Keely gave him a dreamy smile and said, "Don't just stand there. Come inside."

Heart bursting with love, he climbed the concrete steps, each one taking him closer to the beautiful woman with the long, gorgeous red hair and sea-green eyes who would soon be his wife.

Today, he would make their engagement official, by sliding his grandmother's ring onto her finger.

Keely stepped aside and Ethan moved deeper into the house. He set the puppy on the ground and gave the hand signal to stay. Cupcake sat obediently at Ethan's feet.

Baloo did the same.

"Where's Flicka?" he whispered.

"Waiting for us in the living room, all but busting with impatience."

"Wait." He stopped her from turning away with a hand on her arm. "I want to give you your Christmas present first."

"Now?"

"Definitely now." He slid the antique, two-carat diamond ring onto her finger. It was a perfect fit.

"Oh, Ethan. It's…it's beautiful. I love it." She lifted misty eyes to his face. "I love you."

"I love you more."

She yanked him against her and kissed him hard on the lips. "Well, I love you most."

He laughed, knowing his life with this woman would be chaotic and loving and full of challenges. He wouldn't want it any other way. "Fair warning, Ms. O'Toole, I'm not a fan of long engagements."

"That makes two of us."

They were finally on the same page, for all the

right reasons, ready to step into the future together, as husband and wife. After another, longer kiss, the puppy lost his patience and barked.

"Is that Dr. Ethan and Baloo?" Flicka called out.

"It is," Keely called back. "And they brought your Christmas present with them."

"Really? What is it?"

"Come see for yourself."

Pounding feet sounded seconds before Flicka entered the mudroom. Her shriek of pure delight had both dogs barking and Ethan resisting the urge to cover his ears.

The little girl kissed Baloo on the head, then dropped to her knees in front of the puppy. She touched the big red bow around his neck. "Is…is he for me?"

"Merry Christmas, Flicka."

She burst into tears, which set off more barking and a canine lovefest. Baloo nuzzled Flicka's cheek. The puppy licked her face.

Sighing over the happy scene, Keely looped her arm through his. "Merry Christmas, Dr. Scott."

"Merry Christmas."

They moved the celebration into the living room, where they spent the rest of the morning laughing, eating cookies and opening presents. The dogs focused all their efforts on pile-driving through the discarded wrapping paper and boxes.

The sweet chaos filled Ethan with unspeakable joy. After losing one family, the Lord had blessed him with another. He would never forget Tracy and Samantha, they would live in his heart forever, but this was where he now belonged.

He was home, ready to begin the rest of his life with Keely by his side and Flicka in their home for however long that turned out to be.

Ethan couldn't have wished for a better Christmas gift.

* * * * *

Dear Reader,

I hope you enjoyed spending time in Village Green with Ethan and Keely. They certainly had a bumpy road on their way to happily ever after, but they learned a lot from each other. Some of the lessons were life altering, others just pure fun. Ethan even taught Keely how to make snow ice cream. If you've never made this wintry treat, it's fun and easy. Here's a quick, five-minute recipe you can try yourself (*consume fresh snow at your own risk).

Prep time: 5 minutes

Ingredients:
8 cups clean, fresh snow;
1 can sweetened condensed milk;
1 teaspoon vanilla; sprinkles (optional)

Directions:
Place snow in a large bowl. Pour the sweetened condensed milk on top. Add vanilla. Whisk until mixture is creamy. Top with sprinkles if so desired. Serve immediately.

It's really that simple. Enjoy!

I have many more stories left to write. Keep checking my website www.reneeryan.com and Facebook page ReneeRyanBooks for future titles.

In the meantime, HAPPY READING!

Renee

LARGER-PRINT BOOKS!

GET 2 FREE
LARGER-PRINT NOVELS
PLUS 2 FREE
MYSTERY GIFTS

Love Inspired®
SUSPENSE
RIVETING INSPIRATIONAL ROMANCE

Larger-print novels are now available...

YES! Please send me 2 FREE LARGER-PRINT Love Inspired® Suspense novels and my 2 FREE mystery gifts (gifts are worth about $10). After receiving them, if I don't wish to receive any more books, I can return the shipping statement marked "cancel." If I don't cancel, I will receive 4 brand-new novels every month and be billed just $5.49 per book in the U.S. or $5.99 per book in Canada. That's a savings of at least 19% off the cover price. It's quite a bargain! Shipping and handling is just 50¢ per book in the U.S. and 75¢ per book in Canada.* I understand that accepting the 2 free books and gifts places me under no obligation to buy anything. I can always return a shipment and cancel at any time. Even if I never buy another book, the two free books and gifts are mine to keep forever.

110/310 IDN GH6P

Name	(PLEASE PRINT)

Address		Apt. #

City	State/Prov.	Zip/Postal Code

Signature (if under 18, a parent or guardian must sign)

Mail to the **Reader Service:**
IN U.S.A.: P.O. Box 1867, Buffalo, NY 14240-1867
IN CANADA: P.O. Box 609, Fort Erie, Ontario L2A 5X3

**Are you a current subscriber to Love Inspired® Suspense books
and want to receive the larger-print edition?
Call 1-800-873-8635 or visit www.ReaderService.com.**

* Terms and prices subject to change without notice. Prices do not include applicable taxes. Sales tax applicable in N.Y. Canadian residents will be charged applicable taxes. Offer not valid in Quebec. This offer is limited to one order per household. Not valid for current subscribers to Love Inspired Suspense larger-print books. All orders subject to credit approval. Credit or debit balances in a customer's account(s) may be offset by any other outstanding balance owed by or to the customer. Please allow 4 to 6 weeks for delivery. Offer available while quantities last.

Your Privacy—The Reader Service is committed to protecting your privacy. Our Privacy Policy is available online at www.ReaderService.com or upon request from the Reader Service.

We make a portion of our mailing list available to reputable third parties that offer products we believe may interest you. If you prefer that we not exchange your name with third parties, or if you wish to clarify or modify your communication preferences, please visit us at www.ReaderService.com/consumerschoice or write to us at Reader Service Preference Service, P.O. Box 9062, Buffalo, NY 14240-9062. Include your complete name and address.

LISLP15

REQUEST YOUR FREE BOOKS!
2 FREE WHOLESOME ROMANCE NOVELS
IN LARGER PRINT
PLUS 2
FREE
MYSTERY GIFTS

✺✺✺✺✺✺✺✺✺✺✺✺✺✺✺✺✺✺✺✺✺✺

HEARTWARMING™

❧❧❧❧❧❧❧❧❧❧❧❧❧❧❧❧❧❧❧❧❧❧

Wholesome, tender romances

YES! Please send me 2 FREE Harlequin® Heartwarming Larger-Print novels and my 2 FREE mystery gifts (gifts worth about $10). After receiving them, if I don't wish to receive any more books, I can return the shipping statement marked "cancel." If I don't cancel, I will receive 4 brand-new larger-print novels every month and be billed just $5.24 per book in the U.S. or $5.99 per book in Canada. That's a savings of at least 19% off the cover price. It's quite a bargain! Shipping and handling is just 50¢ per book in the U.S. and 75¢ per book in Canada.* I understand that accepting the 2 free books and gifts places me under no obligation to buy anything. I can always return a shipment and cancel at any time. Even if I never buy another book, the two free books and gifts are mine to keep forever.

161/361 IDN GHX2

Name   (PLEASE PRINT)

Address   Apt. #

City   State/Prov.   Zip/Postal Code

Signature (if under 18, a parent or guardian must sign)

Mail to the **Reader Service:**
IN U.S.A.: P.O. Box 1867, Buffalo, NY 14240-1867
IN CANADA: P.O. Box 609, Fort Erie, Ontario L2A 5X3

* Terms and prices subject to change without notice. Prices do not include applicable taxes. Sales tax applicable in N.Y. Canadian residents will be charged applicable taxes. Offer not valid in Quebec. This offer is limited to one order per household. Not valid for current subscribers to Harlequin Heartwarming larger-print books. All orders subject to credit approval. Credit or debit balances in a customer's account(s) may be offset by any other outstanding balance owed by or to the customer. Please allow 4 to 6 weeks for delivery. Offer available while quantities last.

Your Privacy—The Reader Service is committed to protecting your privacy. Our Privacy Policy is available online at www.ReaderService.com or upon request from the Reader Service.

We make a portion of our mailing list available to reputable third parties that offer products we believe may interest you. If you prefer that we not exchange your name with third parties, or if you wish to clarify or modify your communication preferences, please visit us at www.ReaderService.com/consumerschoice or write to us at Reader Service Preference Service, P.O. Box 9062, Buffalo, NY 14240-9062. Include your complete name and address.

READERSERVICE.COM

Manage your account online!

- Review your order history
- Manage your payments
- Update your address

> *We've designed the*
> *Reader Service website*
> *just for you.*

Enjoy all the features!

- Discover new series available to you, and read excerpts from any series.
- Respond to mailings and special monthly offers.
- Connect with favorite authors at the blog.
- Browse the Bonus Bucks catalog and online-only exculsives.
- Share your feedback.

Visit us at:

ReaderService.com